"You shouldn't be here."

Thaddeus had to yell to be heard over the sound of the idling plane engine and the streaming wind.

Monica's dark eyes snapped with anger and a trace of exhaustion. "Neither should you."

"Get back on the plane." He'd have picked her up and deposited her there himself, but that would require touching her—something he was loath to do. The woman had long ago proven irresistible to him. He didn't need to get any closer to her than he already was.

"I've traveled too far to turn around now." Her words sounded worn-out, as though she'd repeated them to herself many times.

His heart gave a sympathetic lurch, which he instinctively resisted. He couldn't let this woman get under his skin—she'd done it once before, and it had taken him all of the past six years to get over her. "Get back on the plane. The fog is getting worse. If you don't leave now, you might not be able to leave for days."

"I'm not leaving without you."

Books by Rachelle McCalla

Love Inspired Suspense

Survival Instinct
Troubled Waters
Out on a Limb
Danger on Her Doorstep
Dead Reckoning
**Princess in Peril*
**Protecting the Princess*
The Detective's Secret Daughter
**Prince Incognito*
**The Missing Monarch*

*Reclaiming the Crown

RACHELLE McCALLA

is a mild-mannered housewife, and the toughest she ever has to get is when she's trying to keep her four kids quiet in church. Though she often gets in over her head, as her characters do, and has to find a way out, her adventures have more to do with sorting out the carpool and providing food for the potluck. She's never been arrested, gotten in a fistfight or been shot at. And she'd like to keep it that way! For recipes, fun background notes on the places and characters in this book and more information on forthcoming titles, visit www.rachellemccalla.com.

THE MISSING MONARCH

RACHELLE McCALLA

Love Inspired

Recycling programs for this product may not exist in your area.

ISBN-13: 978-0-373-67527-2

THE MISSING MONARCH

This edition published by arrangement with Love Inspired Books.

www.LoveInspiredBooks.com

Printed in U.S.A.

Seek first his kingdom and his righteousness,
and all these things will be given to you as well.

—*Matthew* 6:33

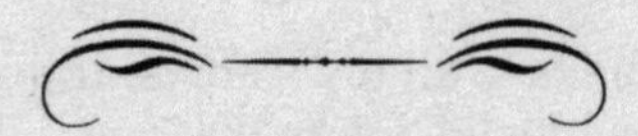

To Henry, my firstborn,
valiant protector of the realm. I love you.

Acknowledgments

Special thanks to all my readers. If this is your first visit to Lydia, I pray that you will love it enough to seek out the stories that have come before. And if you've stayed with these siblings through all the trials of their adventures, I pray you'll find their journey an encouragement on your own.

ONE

"Regis?"

The Crown Prince Thaddeus of Lydia didn't hesitate to respond to his prearranged code name. "Yes?"

"Have you seen the news?"

"Always."

"Then you know—?"

"Yes." Thaddeus didn't need his friend Kirk, the sole person on earth who knew how to reach him, to elaborate any more over the phone. Yes, he knew that the tiny kingdom of Lydia had been nearly overtaken by insurgent forces ten days before. He also knew who was behind those forces—a man who went by the code name 8, short for Octavian, an egomaniac would-be despot, who'd stop at nothing to achieve the power he desired. What Thad didn't know, was how to stop him from taking over the tiny kingdom.

"You know that we need you?" A voice broke in, a female. One of his sisters? Princess Isabelle or Princess Anastasia, he couldn't be sure which one.

"You need me to stay right where I am." Thad hoped his sister could hear the authority in his voice. He was, after all, her big brother, besides being the crown prince of the Christian nation. He knew what he was talking about.

"No—" Isabelle's voice for sure. "We need you on the thr—"

"Don't say it." Thad interrupted her before she could drop any words that might give away his identity. They had no way of being certain their line was secure, though he knew Kirk would have taken every possible precaution. The risk was simply too great. If Octavian ever found where he was hiding, all the sacrifices he'd made would have been in vain.

"We need you here." That was Alexander's voice, so much more mature than when Thad had left home. But then, Prince Alexander had been through many trials on behalf of Lydia. "You're the only one who can end this."

"If I come home, things will only get worse, I promise you. You have to trust that I know what I'm talking about."

"If you would explain—"

"I can't. Not over the phone. You know that." Thad took a deep breath, wishing there were some way he could impress upon his younger siblings the gravity of the situation. They couldn't underestimate the foe they were up against. "Please don't try to contact me again. The risks are far too great."

"You need to come home." It was Kirk's voice again, insistent this time.

"No. I need to go. Goodbye." Thad gripped the phone, knowing he needed to end the call and cut the line that exposed him to potential detection. Still, he hesitated to sever the connection to his family. He missed them so much, the six long years since he'd seen them last weighing on his heart.

Anastasia's voice echoed distantly over the still-live line. "You were right, Kirk. He's determined not to return. I wish we could make him understand, but we can't risk trying to visit him, and he won't listen to any of us."

"There is one person he might listen to. I don't know if I can convince her—"

"Don't!" Thad nearly shouted, glad he hadn't hung up the phone after all. "Don't bring her into this. Never speak of her again."

"But—"

"No. There's nothing she can say to me that will change anything. She deserves her privacy. Do you understand?" Silence ticked by in tense seconds, and Thad feared the connection had been severed after all. "Promise me you won't try to contact her."

Reluctance filled Kirk's voice. "I promise."

"Thank you. I've got to go." Thad ended the call, feeling even more alone than he had mere moments before, the reminder of his long-lost wife prickling the long-dead parts of his heart like blood rushing back to a sleeping appendage, as though to rouse his buried feelings back to life.

He trusted his friend. Kirk would keep his promise not to reach out to Monica.

Thad stared at the phone in his hand, replaying the details of their conversation. They hadn't spoken Monica's name. And surely their line was secure. So why did Thad feel such a breathless sense of panic, as though somehow, by mentioning a woman he cared about, they'd exposed Monica to detection?

Because he knew his enemy. And every time he'd underestimated Octavian before, he'd been wrong. Dead wrong.

"I'll be back in an hour," Monica Miller promised her mother as she headed out for her morning run.

"Take your time." Sheila Miller dismissed her concern. "Peter and I have big plans. We're going to set up a fort in the sandbox."

Monica looked up as she stretched her calves against the shallow step that topped the graceful sidewalk in front of her modest Seattle bungalow. "You spoil him," she accused with a smile.

"I'm his grandmother. It's my job." Sheila wrapped her arms around Peter and kissed the blond curls atop the young boy's head.

"Thank you, Mom. I love you both!" Monica called over her shoulder as she took off down the familiar sidewalk of her friendly neighborhood. The

June morning was still a little cool—perfect for her workout. Even more perfect, her mother had offered to watch Peter every morning as Monica finished her marathon training.

Inhaling deeply, Monica thanked God for the blessings in her life. Her son. Her parents, who loved their five-year-old grandson and had never pressured her to tell them who his father was.

Which was a good thing, because she couldn't tell them. They'd never met Crown Prince Thaddeus of Lydia and would probably have a difficult time digesting her story about their whirlwind romance, secret elopement and—hardest of all—his sudden disappearance before she'd even realized she was pregnant.

Truth be told, *she* didn't really understand why Thad had left her, but she trusted him enough to obey his order never to look for him. From what she'd seen on the news lately about the troubles in that tiny Mediterranean kingdom, Thad had been right about his dangerous enemies. Lydia's government had nearly been toppled.

For the first time, Monica had felt a tiny glimmer of gratitude that Thad hadn't brought her home to Lydia after all. Though she'd have rather grown old with her husband by her side, she appreciated the freedom to finish her degree and follow her dreams of becoming a professor of foreign languages. And Peter was growing up in a safe place. Her son's safety and well-being was more important to her than anything. To preserve that, she was willing to live out the rest of her life in the lonely limbo of technically married, but functionally single.

Monica rounded a corner to a tree-lined street as she followed her daily running circuit.

An unfamiliar car pulled up beside her, rolling at a creeping pace that matched her jogging speed.

Monica glanced at it. Did she know these people? She'd had friends stop to chat before, and the youth from church loved nothing more than to honk and wave frantically whenever they saw her out for a run.

Dark-tinted windows hid whoever was inside.

She picked up her pace, nearly sprinting.

The car sped up with her. Suddenly both passenger's side doors opened and two men leaped out.

Monica tried to scream, but one man covered her mouth with an odorous cloth, scooping her up by her shoulders while the other picked her up by her legs. Her panic faded as darkness blocked out the light of the sun.

"We've got a seaplane taxiing toward the personnel dock."

"In this fog?" Thad pulled his attention away from the charts on his desk and hurried down the hallway after the oil-rig worker who'd brought him the message. The Prudhoe Bay oil fields north of Alaska were remote, almost unreachable. Deliveries were clumped together and personnel exchanges scheduled weeks ahead of time. No one made the trip by chance. They weren't expecting anyone.

He clattered down the stairs, reaching the landing just as a woman disembarked from the plane. Shoulder-length dark hair blew across her face in the arctic wind, obscuring her features.

Still, his heart lurched with recognition, and he crossed the platform in three strides, just in time for her to brush back her hair and meet his eyes.

Monica.

"You shouldn't be here." He had to yell to be heard over the sound of the idling plane engine and the streaming wind.

Her dark eyes snapped with anger and a trace of exhaustion. "Neither should you."

"Get back on the plane." He'd have picked her up and deposited her there himself, but that would require touching her—a risk he wouldn't take unless he had to. The woman had long ago proven irresistible to him. He didn't need to get any closer to her than he already was.

"I've traveled too far to turn around now." Her words sounded worn-out, as though she'd repeated them to herself many times.

His heart gave a sympathetic lurch, which he instinctively resisted. Had Kirk contacted her in spite of his promise? It was a mistake he'd have to quickly rectify. He couldn't give her a chance to get under his skin—she'd done it once before, and it had taken him all of the past six years to get over her. "Get back on the plane. The fog is getting worse. If you don't leave now, you might not be able to leave for days."

"I'm not leaving without you."

Her commanding tone was met with a roar of interest from the catwalk above, and Thad turned to see a crowd of workmen gathering to watch. Out here on the oil rig, they didn't get much live entertainment. He quickly realized he wasn't going to easily convince Monica to leave—not without some explanation. And that explanation needed to be completely private.

"Fine. Come with me." He pushed his way up the stairs, past the gathering men, barking at them to get back to work, trusting her to follow him. Once free of the crowd, he turned to find her close on his heels. "This way."

As he escorted Monica along the carpeted hallway that rang hollow with each footfall, Thad's heartbeat thundered more hollow still.

How had she found him? Never mind that the remote oil drilling outpost sat far beyond even the farthest reaches of permafrost. Never mind that, under strict orders to keep the men civilized in spite of the inhumane setting, women weren't allowed on the rig any more than tobacco or liquor.

It had been three days since his conversation with Kirk and his siblings. Had they contacted Monica in spite of his request? How long had she been looking for him?

And had she been followed?

He ducked into his office, pulled her after him and closed the door behind them both. Meeting her eyes, he fought the urge to push her away, as far away as he could. For her own safety. And his. And the security of Lydia.

But Lydia's security had been breached two weeks before.

The attacks on his tiny kingdom had toppled his family's government and left his father, King Philip, in a coma, fighting for life. Thad had warily watched the reports on the news, knowing that, for all his power as the heir to the throne, there was nothing he could do to help his siblings. No, if he stuck his head up, he'd only make things worse. Too bad he hadn't been able to make them understand that. Monica's arrival endangered them all.

He kept his arms to himself. "How did you find me?"

"Kirk—"

"Not even Kirk knows exactly where I am." Thad's best friend knew only that Thad was living on an oil platform north of Alaska—a vast amount of space for anyone to cover. Thad deliberately moved between platforms frequently. Even his own coworkers had difficulty tracking him down at times. Kirk could have pointed her in the right direction, but Monica would have undoubtedly had quite a time finding him.

"No kidding." She frowned, and her mouth twitched.

"Were you followed? Has anyone been watching you?"

"If you're worried about Octavian finding me, you're too late. He kidnapped me yesterday morning and sent me on this crazy trip to find you. He didn't know where you were so I had to ask Kirk."

"What? Octavian found you? He kidnapped you?" He gripped her by the shoulders and stared into her brown eyes seeking answers. But instead of answers, he felt a rush of emotions. He wanted to pull her into his arms, to protect her from Octavian. But it was too late. "We've got to get you out of here."

"Did you hear what I said?" Her words came out in a disbelieving whisper. "He *kidnapped* me. He sent me here to bring you to him."

Thaddeus tried not to think about the beguiling way she looked at him through her long eyelashes. He tried not to consider how close her lips were to his. He had to understand what Monica was saying. "Octavian kidnapped you, and then you contacted Kirk. How did you do that?"

"Octavian already had his number."

"How did he get it?"

"How did he find out about *me?*" She pulled her shoulders from his hands and stepped away. "You promised me that if I never spoke your name, never made any effort to contact you, never told anyone I'd ever met you, that I'd be safe."

Thad's mouth hung open. The realization of his worst fear sunk in slowly. Octavian had found out about Monica. He'd used her to get to him.

He'd underestimated his enemy.

Again.

"Octavian sent you here?" he confirmed.

"Yes. He hired the pilot to fly me around until I found you."

Thad looked around frantically. "We've got to leave. We'll have to sneak away and hide somewhere else."

"No!" Monica's voice rose to shouting. "Have you heard anything I've said? Octavian sent me to get you, to bring you to him."

"We can't go to him." Thad tried to shush her with a glare that had sent many a calloused oil worker cowering.

"Listen." She ignored his silencing expression. "Octavian needs your signature. He needs a document that he says you stole from him. He says if you sign it, he'll leave us alone."

Thad knew he had to contain the situation. Not only that, he needed to get a handle on the unfamiliar emotions that were thrashing inside him like the arctic waters during a storm.

Even above the constant reek of oil and ocean brine, he smelled her gentle, feminine scent, and memories flew from the prisons where he'd banished them.

She looked up at him, and he clutched his chest, trying to stifle the aching pain that originated there. He'd tried for six years to cauterize that part of his heart, but one look at her big brown eyes tore open the old wound, proving it had never really healed. Yearnings he hadn't felt in years awakened from their long hibernation.

"We need to leave." She spoke with a note of authority he hadn't heard her use before. This wasn't the meek graduate student he'd fallen for so long ago.

"We do." He agreed. "We need to hide."

"*We* need to return to Octavian." She took his arm and pulled him toward the door. "The pilot said he'd wait half an hour. Thick fog is rolling in—he didn't think he could wait any longer than that."

The tug on his heart was even stronger than the pull on his arm, and he pulled her close to him. "I'll hide you. He won't find you again. But we can't go with the pilot he hired. There is nothing outside of this oil rig that is more important than me keeping my head down."

"Nothing?" Her lips twitched again, and Thad

thought he caught a glimmer of moisture in her eyes. The sight of it tore at him. If there was any way he could have spared Monica the pain of what he'd put her through, he'd have done it. But shortly after they'd eloped in Lydia in a solitary ceremony witnessed only by his trusted friend Kirk and the deacon who'd conducted the service, the insulated world of Thad's royal heritage had been shattered.

His father, King Philip of Lydia, had shared with Thad the ignoble agreement he'd struck with the billionaire Octavian. There was nothing his father could have done to change what had happened. After grilling his father on possible solutions, Thad had finally concluded the only way to keep all his loved ones safe and the tiny kingdom of Lydia free from the hands of a deluded would-be despot, was for him to leave.

He repeated his answer. "Nothing."

Monica felt dizzy. Maybe it was a lingering effect from the plane ride, maybe the result of being awake for the past thirty-six hours straight, or maybe the rig itself was moving with the rocking waves.

She'd tried to talk that madman Octavian out of his plan. She hadn't wanted to make this trip, but her life—and her son's—were on the line. She struggled to recall everything Octavian had told her. The man had three objectives to achieve. If she wanted to get home to her little boy, she had to do as he asked.

"Thad, listen. Your father's in a coma."

"I know that." An emotion flickered in his eyes. The thick mountain-man beard that covered most of his face made him almost unrecognizable, except for his eyes. After the many years they'd spent as friends, and the short weeks of love they'd shared afterward, she knew those eyes well. How long had she silently admired this man, content to be close friends, before he'd finally acted on the simmering attraction between them? How many years had she wanted to look into his eyes, content to catch friendly glimpses and look away before her true feelings were exposed? Mere weeks before graduation, Thad had finally realized that their friendship was something much deeper, and they'd gazed into each other's eyes until she'd memorized every glimmer that hid there. She'd lost herself, staring into those eyes years before. She could lose herself there again if she wasn't careful.

"Your father was missing for almost a week. The cr—"

Thad gave her a look that silenced her. She gulped a breath, took a step closer to him and spoke in a rushed whisper. "The crown has passed from him, and he can't be king anymore. *You're* his successor."

"Parliament formed an oligarchy to rule for now. My sisters are a part of it. It's fine." Thad's words were mostly silence and crisp articulations punctuated by anger.

"It's not fine. Octavian wants you to—"

"I refuse to do anything Octavian asks me to do."

Monica realized her hands were in fists. She slowly unclenched them, thinking of Peter. Octavian knew about Peter—he'd even given her the opportunity to call her mother and leave a cryptic message about having to go away on urgent unexpected business for a while. Her mother had been confused and concerned, but happy enough about spending more time with her grandson.

Peter was in good hands. He'd be safe—as long as she could convince Thad that he needed to cooperate with Octavian. She had to make Thad understand. But the last thing she wanted to do was tell him about Peter like this.

She had to make him see that Octavian's way made sense. "The oligarchy was intended to be only a temporary solution until the rightful heir could be determined."

Thad crossed his arms over his broad chest. "It's simple. They can crown Alexander. He's the oldest after me. He's a perfectly capable leader."

"But your father didn't name Alexander his successor. He named you. Unless you renounce your claim to the throne—"

"In order for my renunciation to be recognized, I would have to travel in person—"

"Precisely. If you don't intend to rule—"

"I don't intend to appear publically—"

"You *have* to—"

"They can declare me legally dead." Thad's voice boomed, silencing their war of whispers.

She stared at him. No, maybe those weren't Thad's eyes after all. Maybe this person in Thad's body was someone she didn't know anymore. "You're *not* dead."

But the stranger's eyes bored into hers with a foreign sameness that gave her chills. He leaned close and whispered with intense authority, "The Crown Prince Thaddeus of Lydia is dead. I am Thad Miller, an engineer who left his wife to work in the oil fields of Alaska."

Monica pressed her back against the wall and studied the stranger who looked so much like the man she'd once loved. He had Thad's tall stature, his booming voice. He had the same blue eyes, but the sorrow that simmered in their depths was utterly foreign to her, as was his thick beard, his unruly hair and his attitude.

The Thad she'd once known would never have uttered any sort of lie. Certainly not about something as critical as whether he was even alive. But then, this Thad seemed to honestly believe the man he'd once been was buried and gone, and could never rise again.

A hot lump burned in her throat, and she bit back the reminder of all she'd lost. Her husband. Her life's love. Her son's father.

Octavian had given her more to say, but in the face of this unexpected stranger, she realized those words belonged in another world—a world that still cared about rules of succession and time-honored traditions, and the sanctity of life and death.

She'd gotten a hint of it, traveling from oil rig to oil rig, of the desolation the men endured working there, living off the dregs of greed at the edge of the earth. What had they told her time and again? Most men worked in two week shifts—on the rig for two weeks, and then back to civilization and their families for two weeks. It was the only way to keep them sane.

If a man missed his shift swap, he'd be near buggy by the time he got off the rig. Men did desperate things, and went near suicidal under those conditions. It wasn't any way to live. Not for a few weeks. Certainly not for six years straight. But Thad, as so many had noted every time she'd asked for him, didn't seem to be a man at all. Instead of rotating off the rigs, he hopped from rig to rig.

Never stopping. Never resting.

More like a machine than a man.

Maybe the man she'd married was gone. But that didn't change the threat to her son.

"If you don't cooperate, Octavian has threatened to hurt my family."

"Why would he do that? There's nothing he could gain from that."

Monica forced herself to breathe in and out slowly. Steadily. Thad would be thinking only of her parents and sister. Though he'd never met them personally, she'd spoken of them often enough. Her father was a medical doctor. Her mother had been a nurse decades before, but ever since Monica's birth, Sheila Miller was mostly an at-home mom and volunteer of the year at half a dozen different places. And Monica's little sister was a lawyer—perfectly capable of defending herself.

No, she wasn't too worried about them. Lydia's enemies had little reason to go after them—not when she had a more vulnerable relative with closer ties to Thad's country.

She had no other option but to tell him. Her son's life depended on it. Her hand shook as she pulled out the pictures of Peter. "We have a son."

Thad's face blanched white under his beard, and he seemed to stop breathing for several long seconds as he stared at the pictures with unblinking eyes. "No." He closed his eyes firmly, as though to shut out the evidence she held in her hand.

Monica waited patiently for him to open his eyes again, to take in the images of the child who strongly took after his father. "His name is Peter." She quoted the name she knew her husband loved, his favorite apostle from the Bible. "He's five years old—almost five and a half, as he tells everyone whenever they ask. He has your eyes." She looked him full in the face, comparing him to the photographs of Peter. "Almost your eyes—his are a little more greenish-blue."

Thad reached for the pictures with trembling hands, but then drew back as if touching the photographs would confirm a truth he didn't want to accept. "No."

But Monica could see that he'd spotted the resemblance. She watched the truth sink in. "Peter is your son."

Still he shook his head. "No, no, no," he stuttered mournfully, no longer protesting the truth of what she'd said, but rather, expressing deep regret that it was true.

She'd told herself he wouldn't likely be happy about the news, but his response—utterly appalled—cut at her heart. She loved her son more than anything.

Thad looked as though he wished the boy had never been born. "This changes everything." He looked weary, almost sorrowful.

His expression pierced her heart, but she leaped on the hope he offered her with his words. "So, you'll come with me?"

"Where is he?"

"Peter? He's staying with my parents in Seattle."

"Octavian knows he's my son?"

She didn't know how Octavian had figured it out—unless he'd only guessed. But even if it had been only a guess, she'd already confirmed the truth with her terrified reaction to Octavian's barrage of questions. "Yes."

The sorrowful look in Thad's eyes glimmered with fear, and Monica felt an uneasy terror grip her.

Thad's respiration rate increased. He took the pictures from her, tucking them back away into her wallet and slipping it inside her bag as though he could just as easily hide Peter from anyone who might be looking for him. "The pilot is working for Octavian?"

"Octavian hired him because of his familiarity with the area. But I don't think the pilot knows him. He's not one of his men," she said, a sickening fear crawling up her back. Thad acted as though Peter was already in danger. But no, Peter was safe. He had to be. Octavian had said Peter would be safe as long as she did exactly what he'd told her to do. She hadn't agreed to find Thad in order to endanger her son. She'd done it to protect him.

Still, she felt the hairs on the back of her neck rise in response to the panicked look on Thad's face. Thad never looked panicked. Or he hadn't when she'd known him. Now an ominous chill swept up her spine.

Thad's face blanched pale. "We'll have to take the plane. Let them think we're cooperating. With this fog rolling in we don't have any other way of slipping away." He pulled the door open. "We've got to hurry."

"Hurry?" She couldn't be sure what he was muttering about, but she didn't like the sound of it. He strode down the hall, and she had to trot along just to keep up with him.

"To warn your parents."

Fear swept over her as though she'd been doused with icy water. Her son had to be safe. Octavian promised. Peter had to be safe. "Why do we need to warn my parents?"

"They'll have to sneak away with Peter before Octavian gets his hands on him."

"I thought Octavian was after you. He was only threatening Peter to get to you."

"That may have been what he told you, but if he hasn't figured it out already, it won't be long before Octavian realizes the legal loophole Peter has created." Thad spun around in the empty hallway and, almost as though he feared the very walls might overhear, he leaned close to her ear and whispered, "I've been living in self-imposed exile in order to keep Lydia out of the hands of an evil madman. But if I have a son, they don't even need me."

She felt a wordless plea rise up inside her, that God would take away the words she feared her husband was about to speak. Her fear for her son's safety drowned out any comfort she might have felt being so close to her husband.

Thad pulled away just enough to meet her eyes. "All they have to do is get their hands on my son."

TWO

Thad packed a bag in seconds and threw it over his shoulder before leading Monica down the hallway at nearly a run.

Octavian wanted control of Lydia. He'd hatched so many plots over the years in an attempt to get his way, but all of them had one thing in common: taking advantage of the most vulnerable member of the royal family to capitalize on their connection to the crown. Octavian had first approached Thad's father, Philip, right after he'd been crowned king, while he was still mourning the sudden death of his own parents and wondering whether he had what it took to rule.

That time Octavian's plans had very nearly worked.

When Thad had thwarted Octavian by running away instead of following through with his part of the arrangement Octavian had made with Philip, the ruthless would-be ruler had simply changed his target. Octavian had tried to marry off Thad's younger sisters in hopes of creating a puppet heir.

He'd finagled his way around an old family connection to change the order of succession.

He'd tried anything and everything, but Thad's siblings had held him off each time.

But if Thad had a son, the Kingdom of Lydia had an heir who didn't know enough to distrust Octavian—a young, impressionable little boy who could be molded and shaped according to Octavian's whims....

Thad launched himself down the stairs to the platform where the seaplane waited. The craft was fitted with landing skids. Though some seaplanes could land on water or runways, he could see this particular plane was only equipped for water landings. He quickly clarified with Monica that they weren't likely to fly directly into Octavian's clutches. "Where did you board this plane?"

"On the Alaskan shore north of Deadhorse. Octavian flew me into Deadhorse on a small jet, sent me by bus to the coast. He hired his seaplane to hop from rig to rig until I found you."

"Good." Thad felt glad for the break, however small it was. They could take the seaplane back to the mainland, catch the bus for Deadhorse and then make a break for it. He'd made plenty of connections in the area over the past six years. He could slip out of Octavian's clutches without too much trouble.

The difficult part would be getting Peter to a safe location. If Monica's parents could hide the boy long enough for Thad to reach him, he could take his son into hiding. He'd drafted contingency plans aplenty for himself. The tricky part would be reaching Peter before Octavian got to him. Monica's parents had no idea what they were up against. Peter would be in a grave situation until Thad reached him.

And if Octavian got his hands on Peter, the kingdom of Lydia would be lost.

They'd have to hurry.

Monica shook as he helped her board the plane, and her hands trembled so much as she struggled to latch her seat belt that the two ends merely clattered together until he reached across her lap and buckled them for her. She cast him a grateful smile.

His heart stuttered at the once familiar sight of her lovely lips arched upward for him. Thad struggled to think clearly.

The attraction he felt for his wife muddied his thoughts. Obviously, that was part of the reason Octavian sent her—to get him to think with his heart instead of his head. As much as Thad wanted to scoop up his family and whisk them away to safety, he had to think strategically. Octavian wouldn't hesitate to use any missteps against him. So much was at stake. His siblings had already fought hard to keep the Lydian crown from Octavian's grasp.

The rules of succession were easy enough to follow. Having been named his father's official heir when King Philip was crowned eight years before,

Thad's line had become the official ruling line. With no offspring of his own, the crown could have passed to his brother.

But not if he'd fathered a child—and in a perfectly legal marriage, no less. He'd been married three weeks before he'd left. Alexander wouldn't be able to take the crown, not if Octavian used Peter to claim it first.

Peter.

The name pulsed through his veins with sickening familiarity. He'd told Monica years ago he wanted to name his first son Peter. At the time, having a child of his own had felt like a distant dream.

Now it had become a nightmare.

If Octavian got his hands on Peter, all the sacrifices Thad had made would be in vain.

"Maybe we should try to call and warn them?" Monica whispered.

Certain the pilot couldn't hear her words over the drone of the engine, Thad shook his head. "I don't know where we're going to hide him yet. As long as Octavian thinks we're playing along, he won't touch Peter. Right?"

"He told me Peter would be safe as long as we do what he says."

"Good. The closer we can get to Seattle before we contact your parents, the smaller Octavian's window of opportunity to take him. If Octavian is watching Peter—and we have to assume he is—anything your parents do might rouse Octavian's suspicions. All we can do now is try to reach Peter as quickly as possible."

"And pray."

Thad shrugged and turned his face to the window, where thick fog obscured any sign of the ocean below. "If you want to waste your breath, go ahead, but don't expect it to change anything."

Monica stared at her husband's profile and wondered where the man she'd once known so well, the man whose faith had inspired and encouraged her own, had gone.

What had happened to him?

Granted, from the moment she'd reached Deadhorse, Alaska, she'd wanted nothing more than to turn around and flee as fast as she could back toward civilization. There was such desolation about the no-man's land, a hopelessness that reeked in the air thicker than the stink of oil. Flying toward the oil platform had felt like falling out of the range of the eyes of God.

"'The earth is the Lord's and everything in it.'" She whispered the first line of Psalm 24, as she had a hundred times on her journey north, reminding herself that there wasn't anywhere on earth that wasn't under the Lord's dominion.

Even if it felt as though God was nowhere to be found.

Had the bleak setting worn away Thad's faith? Or had he left it behind the day he'd abandoned her?

She pulled her wallet from her carry-on bag and looked again at the pictures of Peter, wisps of golden-brown curls framing his face, his eyes sparkling with life.

Was he in danger? Had she put him in more danger by coming to find Thad, even though Octavian had promised the opposite? She wanted to believe that her sacrifices had ensured her son's safety—but what if the reverse was true? Could Octavian be trusted?

Thad didn't seem to think so, and he knew far, far more about the man than she did.

Whatever else Thad knew, he didn't know anything about his son. Based on what he'd said so far, he seemed to view her little boy as a pawn in a power struggle. He needed to see him the way she saw him—as the most precious gift God had ever given her.

"You can keep these." She handed the photographs to Thad and watched his face. It was hard to read his reaction under his thick beard, with his shaggy mane of hair obscuring her view, but she studied what she could see of his face as he shuffled through the snapshots: Peter as a newborn; Peter at age two, going down the slide at the park; a recent close-up of Peter's face, mischief sparkling in his eyes.

Thad nodded, but didn't say anything. He looked back out the window, though there was nothing to be seen outside through the fog. Nor did he hand her back the pictures, but held on to them until the seaplane slammed against the still sea, braking hard as it skidded to a stop against the frictionless waves before taxiing toward the pier. When he pulled his face away from the window and slipped the pictures into his wallet, concern knit his brow.

"I don't see the bus," he told the pilot.

"Most likely left ahead of schedule to get back to town ahead of the fog. No sense risking getting lost out here." The man reclined his seat back and yawned. "We can wait here. Buses come along twice daily, sometimes more. You won't have more than twelve hours to wait."

"I thought we were in a hurry," Thad clarified.

"We were." The pilot didn't look at all concerned. "Now we're here. My job was to get you this far. I don't much care what happens after that."

"But we've got to get to Deadhorse. It's seven miles inland—"

"Thad," Monica whispered urgently, gripping his hands, quieting his protest. "We can go on foot."

"No—"

"I've been training for a marathon. I can run seven miles in about an hour. And you always could out-run me. Let's get going." Concern for her son fueled her words. If Peter was in danger, she'd run all the way back to Seattle if it was the only way to protect him. She couldn't sit still and wait when her parents didn't even realize that Peter might be in danger. Besides, Octavian had said his plane would be waiting for them in Deadhorse. He was expecting them there. They needed to reach the outpost town, ASAP.

Thad pulled her back as she reached for the door. "Not in the fog. It's too disorienting. If we lose our way we'll end up wasting more time than we save."

But Monica wasn't about to be discouraged.

"There's a *road*."

"We can't run on the road. In this fog, if a vehicle is heading north, they'll be on top of us before we see them coming."

"We can run *beside* the road." She let out an impatient breath.

Thad shook his head. "It's not safe. Never underestimate the Alaskan wilderness. It's vast, it's remote..."

"I have GPS on my watch. I've already set Deadhorse as a location. We don't have to worry about getting lost. Let's get moving. We've got seven miles to cover."

Thad addressed the pilot. "We're thinking of striking off for Deadhorse on foot. Is that okay?"

"Suit yourself." The man pulled out a magazine and started paging through it. He didn't seem to care what they did.

But the real question, of course, was what Octavian thought of what they did. The jet that had brought her to Deadhorse required a landing strip to land and take off. Apparently the permafrost was far too uneven to risk landing or taking off anywhere but a designated airstrip.

So she and Thad really had little choice but to get to Deadhorse. Octavian would be expecting them there, bus or no bus.

Her mind made up, Monica disembarked.

"Are you sure you're up to it?" Thad slid reluctantly from the plane behind her.

"Of course." Monica stared for a moment at the stark treeless landscape. A dead fish lay on the shoreline, and she wondered how it had gotten there. Then, just as she was looking at it, the fish gave a horrid, twitching flop. She thought about kicking it back into the sea.

"Don't mess with it." Thad pulled her back as she took a step toward the fish. "It's too far gone to live."

She glanced up at him, and something in his eyes told her he sympathized with the fish. Was he warning her about trying to reach the dead parts of his heart? She shuddered as she checked her watch and turned toward Deadhorse, stepping resolutely across the rocks.

Thad hoisted his bag across his back. "The Arctic Circle isn't to be trifled with. It's bitter cold. We might run into bears."

Monica quickly picked up her pace and jogged

inland. "My son may be in danger, and you're worried about bears?" She'd take on a bear to protect her son. She'd do whatever she had to. Spurred on by the thought of little Peter, she picked up her pace to almost a sprint as the rocky shoreline gave way to turf.

For a moment, she wondered if Thad would be able to keep up, but he quickly met her pace beside her, their bags thunking against their backs with every step, prodding them forward. They ran in silence until her watch told her they'd traveled 1.3 miles.

Then Thad cleared his throat. "You were always a determined woman, but I don't recall you being quite this…zealous."

She glanced at him before quickly returning her attention to negotiating the uneven terrain. "You haven't met Peter."

Thad's sudden laugh surprised her. "Is he even more determined than you are?"

"That's not what I meant." She checked their position on her watch without slowing down, then turned her determined gaze to the unflinching fog before them. "He's worth fighting for."

Thad had to fight to keep pace with Monica as she tore through the fog. Thankfully, he spent a lot of time at the platform gym when he wasn't working. Still it was a jolt to his system, sprinting through the fog-drenched air, wishing he could go back in time and change all that had happened. All he could do now was run and hope he wasn't too late.

Step after step, they hurtled together through the dense mist, which clung to them in thick droplets, threatening to soak their water-resistant clothes, weighing them down. Reminding himself to trust the coordinates on Monica's watch, Thad tried to shake off the disorienting feeling of isolation brought on by the blinding clouds, whose obscuring whiteness blocked out everything beyond the few steps in front of them. The alabaster tendrils stretched like fingers across the landscape, veiling what lay ahead and shrouding their future.

Monica clutched his arm, pulling him back as she slowed to a stop.

"Need a breather?" He couldn't blame her for being tired. She'd set a relentless pace.

But she shook her head and pointed up. "Did you see it?"

"No." Without the steady plod of their footsteps and the rustle of their wet garments, Thad picked up the drone of an engine somewhere in the distance. "I can hear it, though."

"How far away do you think—"

Before she could finish her question, the drone roared down upon them, its wheeled landing gear piercing the fog like claws above their heads.

Thad grabbed Monica by the shoulders as he

flung himself down, landing hard on his shoulder, uncertain whether it was more important to shield her from the hard damp ground, or the threat above them.

The plane swept past them, out of sight again, and Thad pulled Monica back to her feet. He didn't recognize the plane, but it certainly wasn't one belonging to his oil fleet, or the plane that had brought them to shore. "What was that?"

"It looks like the little jet that brought me to Deadhorse." Monica stared through the mist in the direction the aircraft had disappeared. "They told me it couldn't land on the permafrost. It needs tarmac."

"So what is it doing?"

"Looking for us?" Monica's guess sounded frantic.

The roar of the engine grew louder as the plane bore down on them from somewhere in the disorienting fog. Since they couldn't see the jet, Thad realized the pilot wouldn't be able to see them, either. Flying by instruments, the pilot could avoid scraping the earth, but they stood tall enough off the ground that it could crash right into them in the thick fog.

"Run!" He grabbed her arm and pulled her forward. They sprinted at a faster pace than they'd adopted earlier.

Still, Monica looked at him with terror in her eyes. "Where are we going to hide?"

"Just run." He could hear the plane bearing down

on them again. "This way." Tugging her off to the right, he hoped they could lose their pursuers in the fog if they veered off the course of the road. Surely the plane was using the coordinates of the road to find them—the pilot wouldn't be able to see anything through the blanketing clouds.

It was all they could do to keep running for Deadhorse. Too bad the tiny town was still miles away.

Above them the sound of the approaching plane grew louder with its descent, but each time he thought they were about to be buzzed, the sound faded again through the dense fog. Monica's dead sprint lagged slightly. He knew she had to be winded. They couldn't keep up their frantic pace forever.

"What do you think?" She panted, gulping air as she tried to speak. "They can't land that plane here."

Thad understood what she was asking. Even if the plane had been sent by Octavian, what was his goal? They couldn't scoop them up and carry them off.

"The pilot must have told them we left his plane. Maybe they're just trying to keep tabs on us."

"That fits." Monica gulped air. "From the moment Octavian's men kidnapped me, I never had the slightest chance to escape. I've always felt like someone was watching me. It's like he was paranoid that I might slip out of his grasp, even with the threat he made against Peter."

"He's been too close to getting what he wants, and

lost it before," Thad confirmed. "He doesn't want to let us out of his sight."

Moments later the plane bore down on them again, this time from directly in front of them. The whine of the engine grew louder, impossibly loud as it had before. But this time, instead of fading away without a glimpse of the jet, the nose sliced through the air not ten feet in front of them.

"Down!" Thad scooped Monica into his arms as he lunged for the ground.

Light flashed around them, and the sound of the plane began to fade again.

Unwilling to risk standing when their attackers could take another swipe at any second, Thad rolled onto his side so he could see Monica.

"Are you okay?"

She panted heavily, but lifted her eyes to meet his. "A little banged up, but I'll live." Thad leaned toward her, as she sagged forward, still gulping air. He pulled her against the padded arm of his jacket.

Thad told himself the move was simply meant to insulate her from the cold ground while shielding her from the plane above. It wasn't as if he was hugging her. He knew better than to do that.

But as she took hold of his jacket with trembling fingers and clung to him while she caught her breath, Thad felt the long-dead parts of his heart lumbering back to life. He could kiss her lips and still their trembling. He could hold her until her terror faded away.

Thad pulled away. His love for Monica had created this situation. If Peter had never been born, Thad would never have left the rig. What would happen if Thad allowed his old love to be rekindled?

Octavian would use it against him. Monica would be a target. He couldn't let that happen, even if it meant denying the longing he felt.

As he rolled to his side, away from her, Thad reminded himself of the discipline it had taken for him to forget her the first time around. When he'd left her behind six years before, he'd given Monica clear instructions to move on as though he'd never been a part of her life. He'd tried to put all thoughts of her behind him, but in the lonely barrenness of the frozen north, his thoughts had turned to her more often than he'd have liked. In her absence, those thoughts did little more than torture him. But with her here, close enough to touch, even his most deeply buried feelings of attraction became as dangerous as the enemy he ran from.

Octavian had a history of using honorable traits like love and devotion as weapons against those who opposed him. He'd tried to trap King Philip by threatening his family. He'd dangled marriage before Princess Isabelle, like a worm on a hook. Octavian clearly suspected that Thad still had feelings for Monica. That's why he'd sent her.

The stronger Thad's feelings were for Monica, the more useful she'd be to Octavian. The madman would threaten her, endanger her, tie her to virtual railroad tracks like the moustache-twirling robber barons of old if he thought he could use her to manipulate Thad.

Thad couldn't let his enemy have that advantage. The only way he could protect Monica, and ensure the safety of Lydia, was to feel nothing for her.

"Are they gone?" Her words pulled his thoughts back to the present, and Thad realized the sounds of the plane engine had faded while he'd been lost in thought.

"Sounds like it. For now."

"What was that bright flash?" Monica pulled herself to her feet.

Thad shook his head as he rose slowly, his body weary from their frantic flight, and a little banged up from diving to the ground. "Maybe they took our picture."

"Why would they do that?"

"Octavian must have asked for proof that we're still out here."

"How did they find us so quickly in this fog? The Alaskan wilderness is huge. What are the odds that they'd pick us out of nowhere?"

"There's nothing out here but Deadhorse and the road to the coast. They can find those with their instruments, same as you can with your watch," Thad explained, but he still didn't like it. Everything about the tiny jet, from its close sweep above their heads to its uncanny skill at spotting them in the wide wilderness, raised his suspicions. He didn't trust Octavian. At all. "How much do you know about Octavian?"

She checked her watch and began trudging southward again. "Just that he's dead set on finding you. And he's apparently very, very wealthy. I gather he's the reason you abandoned me six years ago? It would be helpful if you could explain more about him." A look of challenge glinted in her brown eyes.

Thad felt it hit that tender spot in his heart. She was obviously angry with him, and resentful that he hadn't explained everything long before. He figured she had every right to feel that way, but at the same time, he doubted there was much he could do about it. The situation was far too complicated.

And the appearance of the plane out of the thick fog only made things more complicated. "If Octavian is watching us this closely, it might be difficult for me to slip away and reach Peter before Octavian makes a move."

Fear rose to Monica's eyes. "You can't let that madman get his hands on Peter."

"I don't know how I can stop him. We're too far away. There's too much ground to cover between here and Seattle, and Octavian has far more resources at his disposal."

"You'll have to go along with whatever Octavian says, then. It's the only way to keep Peter safe."

"I can't." Thad wished there was some way to make her understand. "If I let Octavian have his way, then what? All it proves is that he can bully people, that he can threaten the innocent to get what he wants. It makes him more of a monster, not less. Do you really think Octavian will just let us walk away when this is over?" He gripped her shoulders and answered his own question for her. "It's never going to be over."

"Octavian told me that coming to find you was the only way to keep my family safe." Monica pulled her shoulders free of his hands and broke into a jog, as though the mere thought of their son being in danger was enough to prod her onward again.

It was certainly enough to spur him into a run beside her. "Do you have any idea how long Octavian has known about you? Anyone suspicious lurking around? Any incidents?"

"No, nothing. Yesterday morning, out of the blue a car pulled up and two men swiped me and put me on a plane to Deadhorse. Prior to that, there was nothing to make me think I might be in danger." She looked up into the dense fog above them. "They came out of the blue. And yet, I wonder if they knew about me all along, and were just biding their time...."

Thad's heart rebelled against the idea that Monica

or their son might have been in danger prior to the recent events in Lydia. "No one knew about you. If they'd known about you or Peter, they'd have gone after you long before this." He'd given up everything to keep them safe. And yet, he couldn't deny the possibility that his efforts hadn't been enough. He'd been proven wrong every time he'd underestimated his adversary's reach.

"I want to call my parents as soon as we reach Deadhorse."

Thad's initial impulse was to talk her out of it. "We don't want to draw any attention—"

"What do you think that plane was?" Monica protested. "Octavian isn't taking any chances. If he's watching us this closely, I'm sure he's watching Peter. We've *got* to warn my parents."

Reluctant as he was to admit it, Thad had been thinking the same thing. They couldn't trust Octavian to stay away from Peter. Though Monica's parents didn't have any training to prepare them to protect their grandson, by leaving them in the dark about the danger, they only made it easier for Octavian to get to Peter. Would Octavian make a move on the boy? It was riskier to ignore that likelihood than to act on it.

Thad pulled his satellite phone from the zippered pocket where he'd stashed it. "Here."

Monica slowed her pace. She looked at the phone

and came to a stop, reaching for it hesitantly. "Do you think..."

"I think you're right. I don't like it, I don't know what good it's going to do, but we need to let your parents know to be on their guard—to hide Peter subtly, if they can." He handed over the phone. "Call them."

Monica felt the jolt of awareness that stung her hand as Thad pressed the phone into her palm, but she chose to ignore it. She had more important things to think about. And the anger she felt toward him was far stronger than any lingering sense of attraction.

Dialing her parents' home number, she felt her heartbeat thumping furiously, in spite of the fact that she'd slowed her run to barely a walk. Peter *had* to be kept safe. She clutched the phone and waited for an answer.

"Miller residence," her mother answered with the familiar words she'd been using for all of Monica's life.

"Mom?"

"Monica? Are you okay? You said you wouldn't be able to contact—"

"Yes, I'm fine." Monica cut to the reason for her call. "How's Peter?"

"He's great. He's been swinging on the swing in the backyard all evening."

"Are you in the backyard with him?"

"I was watching out the window while I did the dinner dishes, until just this moment when I answered the—oh. That's odd."

"What?"

"The swing."

"What? Mom, is Peter okay?"

"The swing is still swinging, but… just a minute."

Monica wasn't about to wait a minute, or even another second for an answer. "Mom? Where's Peter? Can you see him?"

"He's not on the swing." Sheila Miller sounded breathless, and Monica guessed her mother had run outside. To find Peter—she *had* to find Peter.

"Where is he? Is he okay?" She met Thad's eyes as she waited for an answer that would assure her that her son was fine. Thad looked alarmed—he'd clearly picked up from her side of the conversation that Peter wasn't accounted for.

Finally, Sheila Miller answered breathlessly, "The back gate is open. There's a car in the alley. They're driving— No, no!"

"Mom, what is it?" Monica pleaded for answers, though she was nearly certain she already knew what her mother was about to say. Thad pressed his head close to hers, gripping her shoulder with one hand while he leaned close to hear what was happening.

A frantic sob broke through the phone, and Monica could hear the breathless panic in her mother's voice as she ran down the alley after the retreating vehicle. “They’ve got Peter in that car. They’re driving away with my grandson!”

THREE

"Get the license plate number." Thad clutched Monica's shoulders as she relayed his instructions to her mother. "Have her call the local police. Get a make, model, color—anything they can use to track them down. Maybe the authorities can catch them before they leave town." Thad felt the futility of his words even as he spoke them. The police wouldn't know who they were dealing with. They'd been outmaneuvered all along. Octavian had probably kept his men watching Peter and waiting for orders to take him.

As Monica repeated his instructions in a choking voice, he pulled her against his shoulder, as though by holding her tight, he could somehow keep his son from slipping away. She clung to him for just a moment before ducking from his hold and pushing him away. She handed his phone back a moment later.

"My mom is calling the police." She glared at him, her eyes red-rimmed, before turning and running toward Deadhorse again, this time in a furious sprint.

Thad hurried after her. "He'll be okay. They won't harm him."

"How do you know that?" She spun to face him, half stumbling over her own feet in the process. "Octavian said he wouldn't touch Peter as long as I did what he asked. I did what he asked. I found you. So why did he take my son?" Monica's voice squeaked with panic.

It was all Thad could do to keep up with her. He wished he could think of words that would reassure her, but he had none. Octavian didn't play fair—he didn't even follow his own rules. The evil man had used Peter's safety to convince Monica to find Thad. No doubt he'd gone in for Peter as soon as he was certain he'd flushed Thad out.

Octavian was hedging his bets. He had both heirs to the throne in his hands now.

The madman couldn't lose.

"Peter has to be okay." Monica stumbled over the uneven ground. "Can you promise me he'll be okay?"

Thad caught her before she fell completely. "I promise, he'll—"

But she didn't let him finish. "What good is your promise, anyway? You'll say whatever you have to." She tore her arm from his steadying grasp and darted off again, her accusation lingering in the air behind her.

Thad wavered for a moment as though he'd been struck. He wanted to shake off the guilt her words heaped on him, but he found the charges stuck all too well. Catching up to her again, he attempted to defend himself. "Peter will be okay."

She didn't look at him, but sniffled as she ran forward. "He's probably terrified." She panted as she strained to greater speed. "I've got to get to him."

Thad was surprised by the effort he had to expend to keep up with his wife. "Slow down," he urged her finally. "It's a long journey. You're not going to be any use to him if you wear yourself out now."

With stuttering steps Monica slowed, and finally came to a stop bent double, grasping her knees.

He thought for a moment she was simply catching her breath.

Then she gasped a tear-filled, wrenching sob and sagged toward the permafrost.

Thad caught her by the shoulders. "He'll be okay."

Wrestling away from him, Monica pushed him back, pounding him in the shoulder, her small fists hardly making a dent past the thick down lining of his jacket. "This is your fault. My son is gone because of you. I shouldn't have come. I should have tried harder to get away from Octavian. I should have told him no. It's your kingdom, it's your problem." She groaned and shoved him in the chest with both hands. "I should have *never* taken a second look at you."

Thad realized she'd gone from blaming him for their son's abduction to regretting ever befriending him in the first place, at the start of their friendship that had led to their whirlwind romance and marriage.

He hung his head. Having reached the same conclusion when he'd left her after their elopement, he'd tried to pretend they'd never been in love. But the pain that stung his heart told him he'd never forgotten. And this new pain—the pain for the son he'd never met, and might never meet, now that Octavian had him.

"If we'd never met, you wouldn't have Peter." His words stilled her fighting for just a moment.

"I don't have him now," she spat back, twisting away with enough force to tear herself from his arms.

He let her go, and watched as she staggered back down the path, running through the bleak fog.

His phone vibrated in his pocket. As he pulled it out, he called to her, "Monica, come back—my phone is ringing. It might be an update from your mother."

The identity of the caller was blocked, but Thad didn't hesitate to answer, relieved when he saw Monica emerge from the fog on her way back toward him, cautious hope welling in her eyes.

But it wasn't Sheila Miller's voice that responded to his hello.

The voice came from his worst nightmares, and echoed with evil.

It was the same voice that had banished him from his kingdom.

"Thaddeus of Lydia?"

He hadn't answered to that name in six years. "Yes?"

"I have your son."

Thad met Monica's eyes for an instant before he had to look away. He couldn't let her read the awful news from his face. Instead he turned his back to her.

Before he could muster up a response, the voice continued. "My plane will pick you up in Deadhorse and bring you to my island. You and your wife must come alone. Don't try to tell anyone where you're going. I'll be watching you closely. Besides, your destination lies beyond the jurisdiction of anyone who can help you." The voice chuckled with far too much pleasure. "If you want to see your son alive, don't miss your flight."

The call ended, and Thad reluctantly pocketed his phone and turned back around to face Monica.

The furious red that had colored her cheeks moments before had drained to stark white. "What? Thad, tell me. Is Peter…"

"Octavian has him." Thad swallowed, the images

of the power-hungry multibillionaire resurfacing from the meetings that had sent Thad running into self-imposed exile in the first place.

"Is he okay? Did you talk to Peter? What's he going to do with him?"

Monica's simple questions echoed through his mind, but he had no easy answers. Was Peter really okay? Thad couldn't say. He couldn't predict what Octavian would do next. How could he try to think like a man so powerful, so relentless, so *evil?*

"I didn't talk to Peter." Thad answered the only question he could. "Octavian wants us to meet his plane in Deadhorse." He shook his head. There was no sense trying to avoid the connection now. Even if *he* managed to sneak away, it wouldn't accomplish anything—not if Octavian had Peter. There was no other option for them now but to follow Octavian's demands.

"And then what? What's he going to do with us?" Monica asked.

"You've met him. Did he tell you what he wants?" They weren't going to get Peter back unless they started moving. Octavian had warned him not to miss the flight. He took a few steps before realizing he'd lost track of the road as they'd run from the plane. He didn't know where they were. He didn't know what to do, or how he'd get his son back. Reeling in Monica's direction, he lifted her wrist and peered at the face of the watch that was supposed to guide them back to Deadhorse.

"I didn't actually meet him. We spoke over the phone while I was on the jet to Deadhorse." Monica jerked her hand from his grasp. "This way." She set off at a brisk walk, not bothering to run this time.

He suspected she was exhausted. More than that, he doubted there was any point in running anymore. And it seemed she wanted to talk.

"I need you to tell me everything you know about this Octavian person who has my son."

Thad struggled to think where to begin.

"I'm serious. We need to outsmart this guy, and he already has every advantage." There was that commanding tone in her voice again, that unfamiliar note that demanded compliance.

"Octavian is the reason I went into hiding. He's a chess virtuoso turned billionaire mogul turned…" Thad struggled to think of how to describe someone so calculating, so determined…so invincible.

"Who *is* he?"

"He's gone by many names. He was born Demitri Hasangjekaj in 1951. By the age of eight, he'd risen to international fame as a chess master, but during that time his parents divorced, and he bounced back and forth between his parents and grandparents, eventually taking his mother's new last name, Korkizoglou."

"Sounds unsettling."

"It was. He was eventually barred from competitive chess because of his violent temper. He couldn't stand losing." Thad had pondered the man's history during his years of isolation, and drawn a few conclusions about the domineering figure. "He still can't."

After a moment's silence, Monica prompted him. "After he was barred from playing chess..."

"He invested his winnings in real estate and the stock market. By some calculations, he'd amassed his first hundred million dollars in assets by the age of twenty-five. The more he gained, the more he wanted. He hates having his whims denied. After clashing with the governments of the various nations where he held property, over everything from building code restrictions to rules about exotic pets, he decided he didn't want anyone to tell him what to do. He's purchased isolated islands all over the world, and applied to the United Nations for membership as a recognized nation."

"What?" Monica interrupted his story. "He applied for *nationhood* status? I thought he was just one man."

"One very powerful man, who doesn't want to be controlled by anyone."

"So what did the U.N. do?"

"After they got done laughing at his request, they turned him down."

"They turned down the guy who hates being denied anything? Please tell me he learned his lesson."

"Unfortunately, their refusal had quite the opposite effect. It galvanized his determination to buy a seat, no matter what the cost. Regrettably, when he first approached my father, no one in Lydia realized what he was after."

"Demitri?"

"By this time he'd decided he was a reincarnation of Caesar Augustus, also known as Octavian. He often goes by the code name 8."

"Probably as a result of having to learn to spell all those long last names as a kid."

"I have no doubt many of his delusions are rooted in the experiences of his twisted youth. Unfortunately, understanding *why* he's so determined hasn't brought me any closer to effectively defending Lydia from him." Thad slowed his steps as Deadhorse came into view through the thinning fog. "If I had any idea how to stop him, I would do whatever it takes. Six years ago, when I arrived in Lydia to tell my parents I had a wife, before I had a chance to introduce you to anyone, my father brought me to the negotiating table to meet Octavian."

Thad's steps slowed to a stop, and he faced Monica with all his regrets. "I was supposed to hand over my kingdom to a man who had no concern for its people. My father got in over his head. He agreed to things before he understood the implications. *He* had no way out."

Monica trembled as she looked up at him. "And you?"

"I couldn't undo what he'd already done, but there was no way I could go along with it, either. I was the next cog in the wheel of Octavian's diabolical plan. The only way I could keep him from rolling over Lydia with the crush of his relentless drive for power, was to leave."

"How did your leaving keep him from taking over the Lydian crown?"

"When I was twenty-two, my grandparents died in a helicopter crash, and my father became king. At that time, he officially named me his successor. My appointment was formally approved by the royal council, and I signed the Article of the Crown, a document stored in the Scepter of Charlemagne. If Octavian were to remove my father from the throne without my renunciation, I would become the next king."

"So, Octavian needs your signature renouncing your claim to the throne."

"Precisely. In order to prevent that, I hid the scepter and left without signing anything."

"That's why you left." Monica's voice held resentment and confusion. "But I don't understand. How could Octavian gain control of Lydia? He wanted to be king?"

"He wanted to *be* king, or he wanted a king he could control."

"So, your father…"

"Octavian first approached my father shortly after he'd been crowned king, following my grandparents' untimely death. I believe my father was emotionally vulnerable at the time, and unsure of himself as a new ruler, so he was easily swayed by Octavian's requests. In exchange for opening factories and financing mammoth building projects, my father granted Octavian royal titles."

"Royal titles?"

"He was first an earl, then a duke, but his requests became more and more demanding. He claimed he'd built Lydia into a financially stable nation through his investments and deserved to be rewarded."

"But, didn't he profit from his projects?"

"Immensely. So did Lydia." Thad kept trudging. "By the time he demanded power over the crown, he and his associates had already been granted enough titles to make him a very influential member of the royal council, which validates the king's successor."

"I thought *you* were the king's successor."

"Precisely. When I was twenty-two, the royal council validated my right of succession, should anything happen to my father. The ruling monarch holds the right to name his successor. Normally there's no question. The ruling king or queen bequeaths the crown to their eldest child. If there were no children to inherit it, the ruling monarch would select a relative, such as a sibling or niece or nephew. The royal council always approves the successor, usually as a formality, as in my case. But in those cases in which the line of succession was in question—"

"Wait, wait," Monica interrupted him. "*You'd* already been named your father's heir. And you have three siblings. How could there have been any doubt—"

"There shouldn't have been any doubt," Thad explained. "That's why Octavian's requests were so irregular."

"So how could there be any question?"

"Given his power over the royal council, all he needed was for me to renounce my right to the crown so my father would name him successor. Then the royal council would rubber-stamp their approval, and he would be crowned."

"But if he had so much influence over the government already, why press for more? Why was he so determined to control the crown?"

Thad had puzzled over the same question for years, and finally come to understand what was driving Octavian. "Checkmate."

Monica stumbled.

He caught her arm, and she met his eyes.

She opened her mouth to speak, but it took a moment for words to come out. "He—he's playing a giant round of chess with your family? He wants to topple your father's government, like it's some kind of *game?*"

"He wants power. He was kicked out of competitive chess, but he still wants to show the world he's the best at the game."

"That's crazy."

"Yes." Thad trudged in the direction of Deadhorse. "He's crazy and powerful and determined."

"And he has my son." Monica's voice dropped nearly to a whisper.

Rather than let her think too much about Peter, and possibly start sobbing all over again, Thad continued with his history of the Octavian's schemes. "I thought by leaving, I'd made a decisive move that would keep him from taking over the throne. My hope was that he'd eventually give up, or at least turn his attention somewhere else."

"But he didn't give up."

"Not nearly. Octavian tried various means to scare me out of hiding, including pressuring my father into putting Kirk on trial for my murder. Kirk helped me disappear and was therefore the last person on earth to see me alive. But I was never declared legally dead, and Kirk was exonerated."

"But that took place years ago. Why is Octavian only coming after you now?"

"Octavian is cunning. He tried other means to gain control of Lydia. This recent ambush on my family has brought to light the many allegiances he has formed in the intervening years, besides trying to gain control of the government through my sisters. Remember, he was a chess master. He is used to thinking several steps ahead of everyone else. I'm sure he has many moves up his sleeve."

Monica met Thad's eyes and felt a cold fear engulf her, as though everything inside her had turned as icy as the arctic air around them. Like trying to run in a nightmare, only to find herself unable to move, she felt helpless, panicked, alone. Octavian was determined and powerful and three steps ahead of them already. And he had Peter.

Monica blew out a long, tension-filled breath. It made her crazy to think that her son was in the hands of such a power-hungry madman. On top of that, she'd always resented how very little Thad had explained when he'd abruptly left her. He'd kept his royal status a secret until just before their wedding. He'd told her he was a prince the morning he married her. When he'd left three weeks later, he'd explained the bare facts in a letter, rather than tell her to her face that he was going into exile.

It was Thad's fault her son was gone. If he'd at least warned her, at least tried to hide her, Peter would be safe. They could be hiding somewhere, together. How could he have left her defenseless in the path of Octavian's determined march for power?

She and Peter were being trampled on the maniac's drive toward the crown.

She crossed her arms over her chest and tried to hold back the tumultuous responses that warred inside her. "My son is gone because of your stupid, selfish—" Unable to form words, she grabbed the front of his jacket and shook him. "Do you realize what you've done?"

"It wasn't selfish. I've been living beyond the edge of humanity in order to save my people. That's the opposite of selfish." His hands closed over hers and stilled her shaking.

Monica tore her hands away. "You *jerk!* You *liar!*"

"I never lied to you."

"In all the time I knew you, in the entire time we were friends, even once we fell in love, you never mentioned that you were the heir to the throne of a kingdom."

"I told you my father was involved in the government."

"He's the *king*. That's not the same thing." Monica had worked out her feelings about his deception over the years since Thad had been gone, and she wasn't about to let him make excuses for what he'd done. "You know what it comes down to, Thad? You didn't respect me enough to tell me who you really were. When I married you, I promised you my everything—my present, my future, all that I am and all that I have. And you didn't even bother to tell me your real name until I was ready to walk down the aisle."

"Thaddeus is my real name."

"You left off the Crown Prince of Lydia part." She turned her back to him and looked out at the bleak Alaskan landscape. Deadhorse sat in a haze of fog in the distance, but there was no sign of a plane. She could only pray they hadn't missed it. "If you had told me the whole truth, my son wouldn't have been kidnapped."

"You don't know that. You don't understand who you're dealing with—"

"Because you never gave me a chance to understand. How can you say that you left me to protect me, when you didn't even warn me—"

"I warned you not to try to find me. How was I to know they'd try to use you to get to me?"

But Monica suddenly hit upon the answer. "They shouldn't *have* to go through me and Peter to get to you. If you hadn't run away—"

"I ran to save my country."

"No, you didn't. You ran because you were scared. Your country needs you. If you'd faced Octavian instead of hiding—"

"Nothing good could come of my facing Octavian. I did what I had to do. I made the best possible choice."

"*This* is the best possible choice?"

"I sacrificed six years of my life. Do you think living on the edge of the earth has been easy?"

"No one's had it easy, Thad. I've seen on the news what's been happening in Lydia. Your brother and sisters risked their lives, your father was shot. Peter was kidnapped. Your son shouldn't have to pay for your mistakes."

"I agree. No son should have to pay for his father's mistakes. I tried to end what my father started."

"You failed."

Thad came around and stood in front of her. She didn't want to face him, but the pain in his eyes pulled at her heartstrings. His eyes were too much like Peter's. And she would never turn her back on her son.

"I never meant to hurt you." His voice had dropped to a rumbling whisper, swollen with regret.

Monica fought back angry tears. When they spilled over in spite of her efforts, she swiped them away, and stepped past Thad toward Deadhorse. "You failed at that, too."

Thad let Monica walk away.

She was right. In spite of all his sacrifices, in spite of his exile, he'd failed the one woman he cared about most in all the world.

He'd failed the son he'd never met.

Somehow, he had to make things right again, but he didn't know how. He'd done the best he could do, made every sacrifice he knew how to make, and things had only gotten worse. It seemed Octavian was going to get his way, no matter what he did. But he would do everything in his power to keep his country safe from this madman.

And he would give Monica back her son or die trying.

Dragging his exhausted feet forward, he caught up to her and handed her his phone. "Here. Call your folks. Let them know what's up."

"Octavian said—"

"He said not to contact the authorities. Your parents already said they were going to call the police. That will only upset Octavian more. Try to explain what's up as best you can, and ask them to keep the authorities out of it. Peter's already out of police jurisdiction."

Monica blew out a long breath and took the phone.

He listened with half an ear as Monica struggled to assure her parents that she knew who had Peter, and she was going to get him back.

"I don't know. It's quite complicated," she explained, over and again.

"Yes," she admitted finally. "It *does* have to do with Lydia, actually. Pray for the kingdom of Lydia, will you? I don't think we're going to get Peter back until the trouble in Lydia is resolved." She let out a very long sigh just as a plane cut through the fog, landing on the Deadhorse strip between them and the outpost town. "Please, I have to go now. Just pray, okay?"

She closed the call and looked up at him with fear in her eyes.

"It's going to be okay," he told her.

"Liar."

Since there was nothing he could say to convince her otherwise, Thad didn't argue. They hurried toward the aircraft and climbed aboard the plane in silence, settling into the bench seat that took up most of the tiny cabin. Monica scooted as far from him as she could get.

The pilot looked back at them, but said nothing before taking to the sky again.

Wherever they were headed, Thad figured it couldn't be too far away. The man hadn't even bothered to refuel.

From what Thad could tell by reading the plane's instruments over the pilot's shoulders, they never left the Arctic Circle. Somewhere between Alaska and Russia they put down on an expanse of land that jutted upward like a rotten tooth in the middle of the steel-blue sea.

Thad reached out his hand to help Monica disembark, but she turned her back to him and hopped out on her own. He stepped down beside her and looked around. In the middle of the gray crags of rocks, an expansive sea of concrete stretched toward a bunkerlike dwelling, its cement sides as bleak as the sea and the dismal sky and the metallic scent of the air.

"Dear God, keep Peter safe," Monica prayed in a whisper.

Thad had hurled enough unanswered prayers heavenward to know better than to bother with something as futile as prayer. But at the same time, he hated to think of his young son being held on this gloomy rock. At best, he hoped the young boy had fallen asleep after a full day of play. After all, the hour was well past midnight, though the perpetual light of the Arctic summer illumined even the nighttime sky with its twilit, green-tinged glow.

Armed guards approached them, their uniforms the same gray as the concrete, the rocks and the thin fog of the air they breathed.

"This way." One of them spoke in a voice devoid of emotion, and Thad stepped forward, tempted to reach for Monica's hand, but she didn't look at him as she followed the guards.

Wide double doors welcomed them into an open foyer where interior balconies circled the antechamber in a manner that reminded him of a prison. Footsteps echoed above them, and Thad looked up to see a man approaching the stairs, flanked by more uniformed guards.

Octavian wore a gray suit. His face was an unnatural orange, his slicked-back hair too dark for his age, his hairline lower than Thad recalled it being at the last meeting. His jawline was tighter, too. So, he'd had hair plugs and a face lift. Thad wasn't surprised. If there was a medical procedure that could make him taller, no doubt Octavian would have had it done.

"You were foolish to think you could run from me, Thaddeus of Lydia." Octavian's voice echoed as he stood high above them at the top of the stairs. "Haven't you realized, I *always* get my way? All you've accomplished with your ill-advised game of hide-and-seek is to make me upset. Now things will be more difficult for you and more painful for your family."

Octavian took a few steps down the wide staircase, and paused. "Now, you have a choice. You can cooperate with me, or you can invite more pain upon your wife and son." He held up a small device, and a light illumined behind a pane of glass near where they stood. In its sudden glaring light, Thad saw a room with a sofa, and the figure of a young boy draped across the pillows.

"Peter!" Monica rushed toward the glass.

Immediately the guards stepped in front of her, their automatic rifles barring her way.

She looked up at Octavian again. "Is he okay?"

"He is fine. *For now.* Whether he remains that way is up to your husband."

Thad couldn't help wondering how the man knew

that he and Monica were married, or how the egomaniac had found out about Monica and Peter in the first place. But that question was eclipsed by his concern for Peter and what Octavian might threaten to do to him.

"Now, Thaddeus." Octavian took a few more steps down the staircase, though he still towered high above them. "You don't have a history of making wise choices, but I'm hoping your time away from civilization has given you an opportunity to repent of your erroneous ways."

Rather than let the arrogant man blather on, insulting him and wasting precious time, Thad cut to the chase. "What do you want?"

"The same thing I've always wanted. I want the kingdom of Lydia." He chuckled and raised his arm, pointing a signal at the guards who barred Monica from getting any closer to the room where her son slept. The men deftly stepped around her, effectively cutting her off from Thad. Now they didn't even have each other.

Thad realized, too late, that he'd found the tiniest measure of comfort having her beside him, even if she was furious with him. Now he didn't even have that.

The grating sound of Octavian's laughter died away. "But before we go any further, I need to be absolutely certain that I'm dealing with the right man. You've evaded me before, Thaddeus. I can't risk that again, and it's impossible to be certain that's you under that beard." More guards entered through a doorway to Thad's left. Octavian addressed them. "Shave him."

Monica watched with eyes wide as guards took hold of Thad, shoving him into a chair they'd carried out with them, tugging his coat from his arms, stripping his torso down to his T-shirt before wrapping a vinyl cloak around his shoulders and grabbing him by the hair, jerking his head backward.

A loud buzzing filled the room, and Monica feared Peter might awaken from the noise. She could see her son's chest rise and fall as he slept. She could only pray that by the time he woke up, she'd be at his side to comfort him and assure him that all would be well.

A man in a white coat took the buzzing clippers and trimmed back Thad's full beard before pulling out two long bare blades, which flashed and glinted as he moved them toward her husband's exposed neck.

If it hadn't been for the armed guards blocking her way, she might have rushed to stop the man from getting any closer to Thad. But as it was, fear kept her rooted in place, along with the knowledge that they needed Thad alive in order to make a deal with him. They couldn't risk hurting him too badly.

Still, she flinched as they peeled back the last of

the hair on his neck, cheeks and chin, down to the bare skin, leaving him looking exposed and defenseless in the unforgiving fluorescent light. When the man who held him back finally let go of the thick mane of his hair, Thad sat up straight, and Monica saw him as if for the very first time.

He'd hardened in the years since she'd known him. The muscles across his chest and shoulders were broad, his cheeks had lost the last of their boyishness, and his eyes glimmered like poured glass from their hard blue depths.

"So, it *is* Thaddeus." Octavian stepped across the spilled hair and glowered down at the seated prince. The madman made a much smaller figure than the crown price, but was bolstered by heeled boots and the presence of his armed men. "The cowardly lion has been shorn. Perhaps we can tame him yet."

Thaddeus glared up at him and repeated his earlier question. "What do you want?"

"I want you to sign over the throne and crown of Lydia." Octavian's smile stretched wide, his teeth glimmering with the same gray-green as everything else around them. "Or I will kill your wife and son."

The muscles in Thad's chest rippled as he strained against the guards who held him back by his arms and hair. Monica feared that if her husband got his hands on Octavian, he might rip him to shreds. But at the same time, she feared even more what Thad might *not* do. He'd run away the last time Octavian had challenged him.

If he ran away again, she and her son would die.

FOUR

Thad struggled to think. He'd given up everything to save Lydia. He'd missed out on the first five years of his son's life, settling instead for a marginal existence in the barely tolerable frozen north. Besides that, his brother and sisters had risked their lives to save Lydia, and his father had taken a bullet to protect his daughters and his country. Thad wasn't about to throw away all their sacrifices by giving in now.

He couldn't give Octavian what he asked for.

Nor could he hand over Monica and Peter. The boy slept peacefully on the other side of the glass, his cheeks rosy with slumber, his belly rising and falling with each breath. Thad's heart caught at the tender sight.

His son.

He'd never imagined that his brief union with Monica would have resulted in a child. Of course, his mind had been on other things almost from the start—how to save Lydia from Octavian, how to prevent Monica from ever being discovered. He shifted his gaze to her face, and he felt longing swirl with his regrets.

Yes, she was angry enough with him now that she'd likely never forgive him. Even if there was a way out of this situation, even if he gave Octavian everything he asked for, he and Monica and Peter could never be a family. His son didn't even know him. And he couldn't blame Monica for hating him for bringing Octavian and his vile plans into her life. But at the same time, his cold heart burned with the bittersweet knowledge of what could have been.

This could have been his family.

They could have been happy together.

But he could see no hope beyond the ugly choice that lay before him.

"Well, Thaddeus? What's it going to be?"

Thad didn't respond to Octavian's prompt. The man already had way too much control over the situation. Thad wasn't about to let him push his buttons.

He scanned the room, quickly estimating the number of guards.

Dozens, at least. And those were just the ones he could see. The front door had swung open via hydraulic hinge, meaning he wouldn't get it back open again without activating the powered switch, probably in some hidden spot inaccessible to him. More than likely the other exits were secured similarly.

Then there was the remote location. Obviously the

only way on or off the island was by plane or boat. He didn't have either. The plane they'd arrived on would need refueling before it could take off again… whether there were more planes stored elsewhere, ready to fly, he had no way of knowing.

The simple fact was, there was no way he could get off this island by his own power. Even if he overpowered the guards and somehow managed to rescue Monica and Peter, even if he found a way out of this prison, he was still marooned on this chunk of rock in the sea, where Octavian had every advantage, from knowledge of the terrain to control of the trained mercenaries who swarmed this rock.

Besides, even if he ran, even if he somehow got away, Octavian would only scour the earth until he found him again. And he'd be that much angrier when he found him. There was nothing for it but to strike a deal.

But what kind of deal could he possibly get? He had almost nothing to bargain with.

Just his signature and a scepter he hadn't seen in six years.

"You want to be king of Lydia?" Thad eyed the egomaniac warily.

"Yes. Obviously." Octavian sounded irritated.

Maybe Thad held more power than he'd first assumed. Octavian's short temper could be used against him. "In order to be king, you need me to renounce my claim to the throne, and you need the Scepter of Charlemagne."

"I know that!"

"I don't have the scepter on me at the moment."

"Where is it?"

Thad pinched his face into a smile. Octavian was an impatient man. The temper tantrums of his youth could still be easily generated. And Thad suspected that he wouldn't be nearly as cunning when he was hopping mad. "In Lydia."

"My men have scoured the country. They've found no trace of it."

"That's because I'm the only person who knows where it's hidden."

Octavian stepped closer, leering down into Thad's face, his breath as putrid as his rotten soul. "Tell me where it is."

"I can't."

Octavian gestured to the guards who held Monica. "We'll kill the woman!"

"I can get it for you, though."

"If you know where it is, you can tell me where to find it."

"It's been so long…I'm afraid I won't be able to describe the spot. I'll have to go myself."

"That's ridiculous. Give me an approximate location, and I'll have my men tear the place apart looking for it."

"I suppose, if you want to risk burying it further… It's located in a rocky, unstable place. If you send too many men or use heavy equipment, you're likely to crush it or bury it forever. Your claim to the throne will be questioned enough as it is. I don't think you're in any position to hazard it further."

Octavian took a step back, his eyes narrowed and darting as he analyzed his next move. For a moment, he fixed his stare on Monica.

Thaddeus refused to let his fear show. He didn't have much to bargain with, but so far, Octavian seemed to be taking his words seriously. The would-be ruler had seen too many of his plots foiled of late. He couldn't possibly have too many backup plans left.

Could he?

"I will send you to Lydia in my fastest jet." The smaller man spoke quickly. "You have two days to produce the scepter. At that time, if you do not hand it over, I will kill your son before your eyes."

A whimper escaped from Monica, and as Thad glanced her way, he watched her raise her trembling fingers to her mouth.

Octavian saw it, too, and smiled. "I will let you take this woman with you. She may remind you every day, at every moment, of the importance of what's at stake, and just how much you will hate yourself if you fail."

"You can't—" Monica gasped. "You can't separate me from my son. He doesn't know you. He'll be terrified."

"What concern is that to me? Nonetheless—" He raised his hand. A light went up behind Peter, revealing a young woman in a chair behind him, looking nervous as she watched over the sleeping child. "I have thought of all this already. You see, I first told this woman that you'd had an emergency, that she needed to come with me to pick up the child. She lured him into my car. She has proven to be very useful in achieving his cooperation."

The light went back down again. Judging from the expression on Monica's face, she knew the young woman. A familiar babysitter? Thad could only imagine the lies Octavian must have told the girl.

"Now go!" Octavian snapped his fingers, and the guards surrounding Thad shoved him to his feet. "You have two days!"

Monica stumbled as the guards pulled her down the hallway. She wished she could break free from them and run back to Peter. Even with Natalie, his favorite babysitter, Peter was sure to feel alone and frightened. For one terrifying moment, it occurred to Monica that Natalie might be on Octavian's side. But when Monica glanced back at the girl, she saw that Natalie's face was stark white, her eyes wide with fear, her entire posture that of a frightened, bullied young woman.

What had Octavian done to her? Had he kidnapped her, as well? Monica could only assume so. But she knew enough about Natalie's background to know the young woman had overcome many obstacles in her young life. Monica prayed Natalie would be resilient enough to stay strong for Peter, to reassure him rather than frighten him.

Thad staggered along in front of her, setting a brisk pace, showing no sign of fighting the men who escorted him down the stark, gray corridor. They passed through several sets of doors, waiting momentarily at each one for the guards to punch in the codes to open them. From what Monica could tell, this Octavian fellow was paranoid on top of being brilliant and endlessly wealthy. But then, having the Lydian throne repeatedly yanked out from under him might have contributed to his attitude.

It didn't bode well for her odds of survival—or Peter's. She was still somewhat amazed to have made it out of the room alive. Octavian must have realized that Thad didn't have a relationship with Peter—threatening his son wouldn't touch Thad's heart nearly as deeply as it injured hers. Her role, apparently, was to play Thad's conscience, reminding him constantly of what was at stake.

No problem. She was ready to throttle him for endangering her son.

They stepped outside into the brisk air. Despite the date on the calendar smack in the middle of June, the air temperature in the Arctic Circle was stubbornly frozen at a damp chill driven by the relentless wind. From what she understood, it was known to snow year round at the top of the globe. The cold that seeped into her bones made that forecast easy to believe.

As steps were rolled into place leading to the jet's door, a man approached.

Thad shook his head slowly. "General Marc Petrela," he greeted him in a cold voice. "I thought you worked for Lydia."

"I work for whoever is in control." The general hardly glanced their way, but addressed the nearest guards. "Tie them up," he demanded. "Tie them carefully. This man has slipped away too many times. He won't get away again. Not on my watch."

Monica braced herself as the men approached with ropes, and none-too-gently bound her wrists and ankles. Then they lifted her clumsily between them and carried her up the steps, plunking her into one of the beige leather seats.

Their mission for the moment accomplished, the guards made for the kitchen at the rear of the plane as though they'd missed a feeding in all the excitement. Monica's seat faced the rear, and she watched them go, coveting their freedom, though she couldn't imagine swallowing anything. Not until her son was safe in her arms again.

More guards deposited Thad into the chair nearest hers.

The general climbed aboard and took a seat where he could watch them, though he left plenty of space between them—almost as though Octavian's scorn might be contagious, and he didn't want to get close enough to contract it.

Thad slumped toward her. Bound as they both were, neither of them could adjust their position freely, so when Thad's cheek landed almost atop her shoulder, it was all Monica could do to cringe and tolerate his closeness.

"They're not going to hurt Peter." The one benefit of his proximity was that he could speak in a near-silent whisper, and she could still hear him.

"Because you're going to stop them somehow, I suppose?"

"No. Why do you think they let us leave so easily?"

"Easily?" Monica gave her bound wrists a pointed look.

"They let us leave," Thad repeated, "because Peter is the most valuable weapon they have."

Monica glared at him. "He's five years old."

"Precisely. He's malleable. They can tell him you've abandoned him, feed him a string of lies and rule through him."

"How, exactly, is that *not* hurting him?"

"Well, they won't kill him anyway. I thought you'd be relieved to hear that."

Far from relieved, Monica felt her stomach swirl with disgust. That evil tyrant would turn her own son against her. She wanted to leap off the jet before it took off, run back through that maze of a building, find her son and carry him away. But there was no overcoming the ropes that bound them, and besides, the jet had already been positioned at the head of a long runway. An instant later the pilot punched the throttle. Monica felt the lump in her throat press against the ache in her chest.

"I would never abandon my son." She'd deny any claim Octavian might try to make, praying that somehow in the course of his first five years, she'd impressed that great truth upon Peter. She turned her head away from Thad and watched the bleak skyline flash past the windows. "I'm not like you."

Thad sat up a little straighter at her accusation. "I didn't *abandon* him. I didn't know he existed."

"You didn't stick around long enough to learn he existed. It's the same thing."

"It's in *no way* the same thing." He slumped a little closer, propping one elbow on the seat rest until he was nearly in her face.

"If you'd known he existed, would you have stayed?" As she asked the question, the plane lifted off the runway with a lurch, and Thad, already at an odd angle as he strained to talk to her, keeled face-first into her collarbone.

"Ow," he muttered from where his face was buried in the excess folds of her jacket collar. He didn't seem to be able to pull himself away without the use of his hands.

Monica wriggled and tried to push him back, but he only slumped lower.

Embarrassed, she tried to tell herself she'd felt nothing at his sudden contact.

Nothing but a surge of conflicting emotions, as the love she'd been denied for six years clashed with her anger.

Finally he peeled himself awkwardly away, and flopped back into an upright position.

"Sit up straight in your seat and you won't get hurt."

"If only it were that easy."

Monica tried to ignore him. Even if she turned to face the other way, she could still hear him breathing, could still smell the reek of oil that inhabited his very pores, as if he were made of grease instead of flesh. And when she looked straight ahead, he was there on the edge of her peripheral vision, a hulking mass of muscled man, so much harder than the youth she'd once been in love with, but on some level, still the same man.

But at the very least, she refused to think about him, and tried to keep her eyes averted, staring instead at the bleak sky outside her window. Her thoughts flew to her child, and she prayed silently that he would be okay, not just in body, but in soul. Natalie would comfort him. Natalie, his favorite babysitter, would assure him that he'd be reunited with his mother soon.

And Peter would believe her. He had to.

Thaddeus settled back in his seat and turned his face toward the woman who refused to look back at him.

His wife.

Whatever her complaints might have been about his abandoning her, it seemed as though the years had been good to her. She was still beautiful, with her dark hair and brown eyes and smile that could melt his heart. Granted, at this close range he could see the beginnings of the faintest wrinkles etched into her skin. But they were laugh lines, highlighting the corners of her eyes and the upward tilt of her mouth, not the dour wrinkles of pinched lips or furrowed brows.

Monica had been happy without him, then. The knowledge swirled in a bittersweet fluttering in his chest. He was glad for her, that she hadn't suffered as he had. He was glad she'd known laughter and joy, and had presumably raised their son with such. But even as he felt comforted knowing she'd found happiness without him, he wished he could have been a part of it. As those laugh lines had etched themselves into her face, he wished he could have been standing beside her, smiling and carefree, as well.

"It wouldn't have mattered." He'd given her question thorough consideration and reached his conclusion.

Monica turned to face him. "What?"

"If I'd known about Peter. It wouldn't have changed the situation. At most it would have made it that much more important that I stay away from you, and you from me, so that nothing like this would happen."

"I disagree." Monica held up her bound hands to stop him from speaking further. "I don't think your disappearance actually protected us at all. They still found me. Octavian has Peter."

Thad didn't like the blame that buttressed her words. He didn't like the situation they described, either. "How is it that Octavian found you?" he mused aloud.

"I don't know." Monica defended herself as if she'd been accused of personally giving away the secret. "I didn't whisper a word to anyone. My parents don't even know anything about you. Peter has your picture by his nightstand, but he only knows you as 'Daddy.' He doesn't know your name."

Thad felt a foreign stirring of emotion as Monica's words evoked the image of the blond-haired boy being tucked into bed next to a picture of his daddy.

Next to a picture of *him.*

"What does he know about me?"

"Just that the man in the picture is his daddy, that you've gone away for a long time and we don't know when or if you're ever coming back."

"Anything else?" Each detail she shared prickled his heart like a painful scab being peeled away before the wound was fully healed. But he had to know what Peter knew. Octavian had the boy, and would soon learn everything the five-year-old could tell him. Octavian would use any information he could against them. Thad was certain of that much.

"Just that—" Monica stopped herself and shook her head.

"What?"

"It's nothing. It's not important."

"*Everything* is important. What were you going to say?"

Her lower lip quivered, and she seemed to debate whether she should answer his question. Just when she seemed about to speak, General Marc Petrela cleared his throat and approached them, standing in the aisle with his arms crossed over his chest, glowering at them.

Thad glowered back. Of his father's three generals, Petrela had long been the one Thad most respected. He was younger than David Bardici and Corban Lucca. In fact, Thad realized General Petrela wasn't much older than he was. But the man had a lengthy record of service in the Lydian army, having risen through the ranks on hard work and dependable leadership. He'd kept his body in top military shape, instead of going soft like the other two generals. On top of that, he was a churchgoing man. Thad recalled seeing him in worship services for years, back when he was growing up in Lydia's capitol city of Sardis.

As his glowering expression stretched to a sneer, Thad realized just how poor a judge he'd been all those years. Sure, he'd respected the general. But how long had the man been working for Octavian?

Plenty long enough for Thad to stop trusting him.

Petrela cleared his throat. "I've been in contact with Octavian. We've ironed out some of the details of our plans. This plane will be flying straight to Sardis. Once we arrive there, we will accompany you to find the scepter."

Thad didn't bother to point out how presumptuous the man's request was. He had no intention of leading these men straight to the scepter, but there was no need to tell them that. "Can you please untie us now? We've reached cruising altitude. There isn't too much trouble we can cause from here."

"I'm afraid that's not possible. Octavian's orders were very clear."

Thad contemplated a few bitter responses, but kept his mouth shut.

The general continued to glare at them, but didn't speak again.

Thad wondered what he was contemplating. Surely the man knew how reluctant Thad was to hand over the scepter, or to lead them to it. Whatever Octavian's promises about letting Peter return to Monica in exchange for the scepter, Thad didn't believe it. More than likely the general and his men were under orders to snatch it away the moment Thad uncovered it. Then they'd have the kingdom and the heir, as well.

Silently, the general turned and went back to his seat.

Thad looked at Monica, who'd closed her eyes, though she didn't appear to be asleep. Thad watched her for a moment, then rubbed his face with his hands and tried to sort out where his dreams of happiness with the beautiful woman had gone so irrevocably wrong.

He hadn't ever meant to woo her. She was just the quiet girl who happened to sit at the desk next to his, crammed into an undergraduate lecture hall. One day, as he'd been doodling inventions in his notebook, she'd reached over and started naming them.

In Latin.

Impressed, he'd jotted notes back, and quickly learned more about her. She was a student of ancient languages, in love with the written word. She wanted to be a professor someday, but Greek was giving her fits.

Thad had been more than happy to tutor her. As heir to the Lydian throne, he'd grown up learning several foreign languages, including Greek and its close cousin, Old Lydian, the language of his people that had only been replaced by English as a national language a mere century before.

Monica had been thrilled when he'd offered to teach her Old Lydian, and had soaked up all the history of Lydia he could share with her, including its roots in the Bible. Never once had she questioned why he knew so many details about his homeland, or why the last name he used was the same as the name of his country.

She hadn't asked, so he'd never told her who he really was. For a few years they were simply friends—not even best friends. Thad had been careful not to get too close to her then, sensing that she was the kind of woman he could easily fall in love with, and knowing he wasn't in any position to start a serious relationship. He hadn't ever intended to fall in love with her. After all, he had a kingdom to get back to, and she had a career as an ancient-languages professor to look forward to.

But as the time had drawn closer for him to say goodbye and return to Lydia, both of them had begun to realize how much they meant to the other. After one kiss Thad had become convinced he couldn't leave her behind. They could elope, and he'd surprise her with the news of his royal pedigree at the same time as he introduced her to his family as his wife.

But he'd been introduced to Octavian instead.

That was where his life had gone veering off track. His father had been dealing with Octavian before that. And ultimately, only King Philip could explain how he'd gotten pulled into the mess. But his father was now in a coma, having taken a bullet protecting Isabelle and Anastasia from some of Octavian's cohorts…and the longer Philip was unconscious, the less likely it became that he'd ever wake up.

And the less likely it seemed that they'd be able to keep the kingdom out of Octavian's hands. If it hadn't been for all the sacrifices he'd made already, Thad might have been inclined to give up. Octavian had his son. He had every advantage. Thad wasn't even sure how he was going to get away from General Petrela, even for a moment.

He needed a plan. A strategy. When they landed in Sardis, Thad needed to use every moment of the precious two days Octavian had granted him.

But how?

If there was one advantage to having one's wrists bound, Monica figured it was that she could keep her hands folded in prayer, even if she fell asleep.

Exhaustion reached its greedy claws toward her, threatening to drag her into slumber, but Monica couldn't allow herself to nod off. She had to keep praying. At first it was just for Peter—that God would be with him, and keep him safe, and unite them once again.

But the more she prayed, the more she realized there were other things to pray for. There was the kingdom of Lydia and the royal family.

And ultimately, she realized she needed to pray for Thad. Furious as she was with him, she realized he'd need God's help if they were going to get their son back. She'd given up hoping for a future with Thad after he'd left her. She'd severed every tie to the man who now sat next to her on this plane jetting away from her son. But, she realized, Peter and Lydia wouldn't be free until Thad was free from whatever it was that encumbered his faith.

As she prayed for Thad, he cleared his throat next to her and she opened her eyes, thinking he might have something he wanted to say to her.

But he wasn't looking at her. He was looking at the general.

"There are some preparations I'd like to make from the air if we're going to be able to retrieve the scepter in a timely manner once we land." Thad spoke in a matter-of-fact voice, without any underlying threat, other than that implicit in the meaning of his words.

The general stood and faced them. Monica had both her eyes open now and watched Marc Petrela as he considered Thad's request. The man's beady brown eyes darted toward the plane's kitchen, where the guards were, then narrowed as he looked back at them.

Monica wondered what he was thinking. Though they'd left Octavian back on the island, in many ways it was as though he was still with them. Anything they said could be repeated back to him by the guards or recorded by some hidden security device. For all she knew, Octavian was watching them on a screen right now.

"What preparations?" the general asked finally.

"I need to talk to my brother," Thad said evenly.

"Why is that necessary? I cannot allow it. You would only plot some way of escaping."

"Octavian has my son," Thad reminded him, anger spicing his words. "I'm not going to try to escape from you. I won't do anything to endanger Peter. But if we're going to get the scepter in the next two days, I can't waste any more time. Let me talk to my brother."

The general leaned forward and lifted his eyebrows slightly. "I can help you."

Monica felt her heart thumping hard as the seconds ticked by. What, exactly, was Petrela offering?

Thad seemed to consider the same question. Tense seconds ticked by.

"I need to talk to my brother," Thad repeated. "If you don't have the authority to grant that request, then let me talk to Octavian."

"I have the authority."

"Then use it."

Monica watched the general's lower jaw shift slowly from side to side as he mulled Thad's request. Then, to her surprise, he almost smiled as he placed his own phone in Thad's bound hands.

"Call whoever you need to. I'll be listening."

Thad wasted no time dialing.

Monica listened as Thad briefly updated his brother on the bare essentials of their situation.

"Octavian found me." He paused. "I don't know *how*. He captured me and Monica. Did Kirk tell you about Monica? Ask him about her. It's complicated. I'll try to explain when we arrive."

Thad paused again, and Monica could just make out a clip of words that told her that Thad's brother, Alexander, had a lot of questions.

Unfortunately, given the way Petrela eyed Thad as though he might decide at any moment to take his phone back, Thad didn't have the luxury of providing many details.

"We've been captured," Thad repeated. "They've got us bound hand and foot and we're headed to Sardis. We should arrive sometime tomorrow morning. Octavian wants the scepter."

Alexander's voice carried more strongly now.

Though Monica couldn't make out the words, she could imagine the protests he'd have. After all, she'd seen enough on the news to know that Alexander, Isabelle and Anastasia had each been through life-threatening trials to keep the kingdom out of Octavian's hands. They weren't likely to allow their brother to simply hand it over.

"Alec—" Thad finally cut his brother off "—I'll explain more later if I get the chance. Have cars waiting at the Sardis airport, enough to transport Petrela and his men."

Another pause.

"Yes. General Marc Petrela. He's working for Octavian. Right now he's guarding me and Monica, supposedly to keep us from running away, though I suspect he's under orders to snatch away the scepter the moment I uncover it."

Thad spoke without looking at the general, but Monica couldn't help glancing at the older man.

Petrela's lips thinned. Monica wondered what the man was thinking. Had Thad's words angered him? Was Thad being strategic, identifying the general's supposed motives, or was he so upset about the situation that he'd let his anger guide his actions?

It was difficult to say which. Thad quickly ended the call and held the phone out to the general, who stepped forward to claim it silently.

Monica watched the exchange. With her son's life

at stake and precious minutes ticking away toward their two-day deadline, she couldn't help thinking that Thad's choices were only making matters worse.

FIVE

Thad rested fitfully over the course of the flight. He knew he needed some sleep if he was going to be able to meet the challenges that lay ahead, but he couldn't rest. Besides the discomfort of being bound, he felt the weight of all that lay ahead. Part of him wished he could go back to Alaska, hide again and pretend that none of this was happening. He didn't want to see the disappointment on Monica's face when he let her down again. And though, as he'd told Monica earlier, he doubted that Octavian would kill Peter, Thad still had no desire to witness whatever mind games Octavian might play with the boy as he trained him to be his puppet ruler.

But at the same time, part of him felt relieved to finally face whatever might be coming in the next two days. He'd felt guilty enough hiding at the edge of the earth. It was restorative to finally get a chance to *do* something, even if whatever he did was certain to fail.

If nothing else, he'd get a chance to see his family

again, to apologize for all the ways he'd disappointed them in the past, before he disappointed them again.

With the risen sun pouring through the plane's windows, Thad realized they'd soon be landing. Sometime during the night the guards had delivered sandwiches and sodas to him and Monica, and they'd eaten as best they could with bound hands.

Monica slept now, and Thad caught himself looking at her again, rememorizing her every feature as he had when they'd been together. His heart burned with a longing so fierce it speared like physical pain through his chest. Then he realized what he was doing, torturing himself by watching her. She wasn't his any longer. It wasn't right for him to look at her. And it wasn't very wise, either, not if he wanted to keep control of his emotions.

He rose on shaking feet and made his way, half hopping, half stumbling, toward the restroom at the back of the plane, balancing himself as best he could against the seat backs with his forearms. Ducking into the tiny water closet, Thad washed his hands and stared at his reflection, squinting toward where his laugh lines should have been.

Nothing. Only the haggard sag of skin under his eyelids, the drooping ridges chiseled across his brow, sorrow instead of joy reflected back at him from every cell on his face. He looked old.

His thirtieth birthday had passed the month before with no acknowledgment, because no one around him knew when his birthday was. And none of those who knew could find him.

It was as though it had never happened, except that he looked as if several more birthdays had passed.

He shook off the thought, splashing cold water on his face and drying it with rough paper towels. This, of course, was precisely why he had to steel his heart against Monica. She made him think about sentimental things like laugh lines and birthdays. She made him soft. Those first few weeks at the oil rig had been the worst, missing her, reaching for her in the night, waking up to find she wasn't there.

If he let himself care for Monica, even a little, he'd fall right back into Octavian's clutches. *This* was why the egomaniac had sent her with him—to weaken him and make him easier to defeat. No, Thad had a duty to the crown of Lydia and plenty of wrongs to put right. It wouldn't do to let his emotions get in the way at this point, no matter how strong the feelings she roused inside him.

Thad lingered in the restroom until one of the guards, apparently concerned that he might be hatching an escape plan from the toilet at thirty thousand feet, rapped on the door and urged him to return to the cabin. As he made his way back down the aisle, he saw Monica's eyes were still closed.

Good. She needed her rest. It was going to be a long day.

* * *

Monica awoke to bright light streaming in through the jet's windows. It took her a moment to remember which flight she was on. Then the recent past caught up to her with terrifying speed, and she sat upright, gasping.

When she caught her breath and looked around, she realized the guards were snoring in the seats nearest the kitchen.

The sunlight streaming in the windows seemed to indicate they'd caught up with morning at some point in their flight, and were likely approaching their destination, as well. Monica found where the guards had tossed her bag, and made her way back to the restroom to brush her teeth and prepare to meet Thad's extended family.

Heading back to her seat, she looked out the window at the island-studded coastline of Greece. She remembered the view from six years before, when she'd arrived in Lydia breathlessly happy, delirious with the wedding plans she was sure would usher in a state of perpetual happiness.

How quickly all that had changed.

As the plane continued its descent toward the tiny Christian kingdom squeezed along the coastline between Albania and Greece, the others aboard the jet began to rouse, and the general stood over them again with an update.

"I've been in contact with Octavian. He's established his ground rules. My men and I will untie you once we land, but we will follow you everywhere. If at any point you attempt to escape, you will only make things more difficult for yourselves and for your son. Do you understand?"

Monica risked glancing at Thad. His expression was stony, unreadable.

"Octavian will arrive with Peter by noon on Saturday. That's tomorrow," the general clarified, in case the long flight had blurred their sense of passing time. "He'll meet us at the palace throne room for the transfer—the scepter and your signature, for your son."

Monica absorbed the news. After accounting for all the time zones they'd flown through and the length of their flight, Saturday at noon was two days from the time Octavian had brokered his deal with them. They'd lost many hours in the flight over, and Octavian hadn't credited them back in any way.

What surprised Monica most was that they were going to be untied. Did Octavian really trust Thad not to give him the slip this time? She'd been somewhat surprised that he let them fly back to Lydia at all. But then, Thad had suggested that Octavian might be just as inclined to rule through Peter as to take the crown himself. And surely Octavian understood that if he was ever going to get his hands on the scepter, Thad would have to have use of his hands.

It wouldn't surprise her if Petrela took the scepter the moment Thad uncovered it, just as Thad had predicted the night before. Or did Octavian have something even more awful up his sleeve? From what Monica understood of the man, he'd quickly concocted plans B, C and D every time his plan A was defeated. Perhaps it was enough to assume their adversary had a pocketful of contingency plans.

In any event, she wished Thad would discuss his thoughts with her. Surely he knew Octavian better than she did, and could guess with more accuracy what the evil man might be up to. Though he hadn't spoken to her for most of the flight, she leaned close to him as the plane began its descent, and asked in a conspiratorial whisper, "Are we going to look for the scepter as soon as we land?"

Thad leveled her a look that sent her heart dipping along with the descent of the aircraft.

"*If* I go to fetch the scepter, I'll go alone." His words were hardly audible, though she leaned close to hear.

"If?" She wanted to shake him, but figured there was no way she was ever going to rattle him enough to make him understand. "There is no *if*. This is our son we're talking about. You've got to get the scepter. It's not optional. Besides, you don't have the choice to go alone." She shot a pointed look toward the general, who'd already promised to follow them everywhere.

"First I need to talk in person to my siblings. They've risked their lives to keep Lydia out of Octavian's control. They deserve to be part of this discussion."

"There's nothing to discuss. You've simply got to do what Octavian says."

Thad leaned forward and dropped his voice. "And what will happen then?"

Monica stared at him, unsure what he was asking, exactly. "Then he'll return Peter—"

"Why should he?"

"He said—"

"Don't ever trust anything Octavian says." The hard look in Thad's eyes seemed to be rooted in experience. "Once he has the scepter, we'll have nothing left to bargain with. We'll be a liability, contenders to the throne who could somehow take it back again. He can't risk that."

"What are you saying?"

Thad closed his eyes as though the burden of keeping them open was too much for him under the circumstances. When he opened them, they glistened with moisture. "Remember back in college, that class we took together on ancient civilizations? What have rival kings done throughout history to prevent their adversaries from returning to power?"

Monica could barely get the words out. "They have them killed."

Thad nodded solemnly.

"But he can't have us killed. That would be so wrong. Surely the world won't sit back and watch as such an injustice is carried out."

Thad looked at her with sorrow in his eyes.

And Monica thought of all the horrid headlines that had told of troubles in distant corners of the world, of dictators and devilish acts performed all over the globe. It happened all the time and left her wishing there was some way she could have stopped it, some way she could intervene to help. Peace on earth remained an unachievable dream no matter how sincerely she and her son prayed for it in their bedtime prayers.

But this time, the injustice was happening to her little boy. Her voice squeaked up a notch. "But Peter is so innocent."

"I know you don't trust me, and you have no reason to believe my promises, but I will do my best to give you back your son."

"Your best?" Monica shook her head. So far, Thad's best had been hiding at the edge of the earth, reneging on his wedding vows mere weeks after making them. And even that sacrifice hadn't accomplished what he'd wanted after all. So far, Thad's best efforts had failed.

The plane gave another lurch and rocked as the landing gear kissed the tarmac. Monica began to wonder if she'd ever see her son again.

Once they'd taxied to a stop and the general instructed his men, he nodded to Monica and Thad and they stood obediently while he slit the bonds that had held them. Then they filed off the plane, with Monica shadowing Thad toward waiting limousines.

A man stood by the cars, and Monica recognized him as Kirk Covington, her husband's best friend from growing up, who'd served as the best man and sole witness of their wedding. There was only one other person on earth who'd known about their nuptials—the Lydian deacon who'd officiated, Dom Procopio.

Thad walked toward Kirk, who'd been accused of murdering Thad, having been the last person seen with the missing prince. Kirk had gone on trial but had refused to say anything about what had happened to Thad. Eventually, he'd been acquitted for lack of evidence, but by that time, he was hated by most of Lydia.

Kirk had made many sacrifices to keep Thad's whereabouts a secret. In addition, if the news reports Monica had watched the week before were to be believed, Kirk had saved the life of Princess Anastasia, Thad's youngest sister, and in the process, fallen in love with the princess. Kirk and Stasi were engaged.

Appreciation welled in Thad's eyes as he approached his friend. Thad glanced at the general, who was still a couple of steps behind him, watching him carefully. Thad seemed to waver, however briefly, over how he should respond to his friend.

Then he stretched out his arms to embrace him.

The overwhelming envy Monica felt caught her off guard. She told herself she didn't *want* Thad to embrace her, but her heart seemed to think otherwise.

Petrela barked a warning as Thad's arms rose. When the crown prince embraced his friend in spite of the general's words, Petrela nodded to his men. Four of them swarmed Thad, grabbing him by the arms and shoulders and pulling him back from Kirk.

Suddenly men in uniforms of the Lydian royal guard stepped out from the other vehicles.

Kirk raised one hand, and the guards paused.

Monica watched the men carefully. They were on Lydian soil. No doubt the Lydian royal guards could easily outnumber the men Octavian had dispatched with Petrela. But if they did, what would Octavian do to her son?

Thad hadn't explained that part to Alexander over the phone. He'd given only a very brief explanation. None of Thad's siblings knew about Peter.

As the guards holding him relaxed their grip, Thad turned around just far enough to face Petrela. "I haven't seen my friend in six years," he informed the general briskly.

"I have my orders."

Thad's expression didn't soften in the least. "We'll be seeing my family shortly. I'll have you know I have every intention of embracing them, as well."

"Octavian didn't finance a family reunion. You are on a mission."

Petrela and Thaddeus glared at each other as though either of them might happily command his men to tear the other to shreds at any moment.

What would happen to Peter then?

Monica stepped in between the men and placed a gentle hand on Thad's arm. "You've got to cooperate," she reminded him.

Anger sparked in Thad's eyes, but he blew out a long breath and seemed to calm down, however slightly. "We have very little time before Octavian arrives for the exchange," Thad reminded the general. "I can't have your men jumping me every time I make a move."

The general didn't appear to be about to back down, either. "I will use my judgment." He raised his right eyebrow slightly. "I'd appreciate it if you would use yours."

"I intend to." Thad stood a little taller, and the guards who held him stepped back. "Can we get going now?"

Petrela extended his hand toward the waiting limo. "After you."

While Thad climbed into the car, Petrela exchanged words with his men, who dispersed to the other waiting vehicles.

Monica and Thad squeezed into one seat together

with one of Petrela's guards, facing Kirk, the general and another guard.

It was a full vehicle. The luxury-sized seats accommodated them, but Monica still felt the press of Thad's body next to hers, and nearly choked on the conflicting emotions the contact generated. She hated Thad for endangering her son. So why did she find it so difficult not to reach for the hand so close to hers, or lean on his shoulder, or bury her head in his chest to cry?

Kirk made sure they were all synchronized at the local time of eight-thirty in the morning, and helped Thad input recently changed numbers into his phone. Kirk looked as though he wanted to talk, but he kept glancing at Petrela.

"Speak freely," Thad told his friend. "Pretend he isn't there."

Petrela bristled visibly at Thad's words, but he made no move.

Kirk gave a wry smile before jumping in. "Your family is waiting at the palace. I told your siblings that you're on your way."

"What about my mother?"

"She won't leave your father's side. He's at the hospital. Since Alexander didn't know much about your status, we all thought it best not to tell her anything until we knew more about the circumstances."

"Thank you. That was wise," Thad agreed. "How are the others faring?"

"They've got a lot of questions about your visit. As you've probably heard from the media reports, Parliament established a temporary ruling council after your father disappeared during the ambush. In order to meet the requirements that the ruling monarch be a descendent of Lydia, they created an oligarchy of contenders to the throne, open to all those with a claim to the crown."

Monica listened carefully, filling in the blanks with what she knew of the tiny Christian nation. The kingdom had been founded by the members of the house church formed by a woman named Lydia, who was actually mentioned several times in the Bible in the book of Acts. The ruling family could trace its roots all the way back through the centuries to the first Lydia, after whom the kingdom was named.

"The crown has officially passed from your father, and by law cannot revert back to him, even if he recovers." Kirk plowed ahead with his updates. "Isabelle and Anastasia signed the oligarchy documents."

"What about Alexander?" Thad named his other sibling.

"I'm afraid Alexander didn't arrive to sign within the time limit set by Parliament, but that shouldn't be much of an issue at this point, since Alexander is now engaged to one of the other members of the oligarchy, Lillian Bardici."

"Bardici." Thad scowled at the name. "David

Bardici, the Lydian general, has been killed, has he not? I caught just a bit of that story on the news. Explain to me exactly how the Bardicis fit into the picture."

Kirk took a deep breath. "At Octavian's prompting, the Bardicis claimed to be descendants of the ruling line from four generations ago, but we've uncovered documents that have disproved that theory. Neither of the Bardicis on the ruling council, Lillian nor her father, Michael, have any actual relation to the Lydian line."

"So the oligarchy council has no basis, then?"

Kirk nodded, regret on his features. "It was created to solve a problem that no longer exists. All that remains now is for the rightful ruler to be crowned."

Monica watched the men discussing the future of the kingdom, and saw clearly what Kirk was hoping. He wanted Thad to be crowned king. With the recently dethroned King Philip in a coma, unable to be recrowned, and without any basis for the oligarchical council, it only made sense for Thad to take the position he'd been born to hold. But Octavian and his determined plans barred the way.

More than likely, Marc Petrela heard the implication underlying Kirk's words, but Monica figured it wouldn't be any great revelation to him.

Nor did Thad respond to his friend's implications. There wasn't time to talk further. They arrived at the palace and shuffled around in the courtyard until

Petrela and his men seemed satisfied with the formation they'd created around Thad.

Then they hurried inside the large marble foyer with its twin staircases curving down, where Thad's sisters Isabelle and Anastasia tackled him with hugs. Petrela's men tensed and looked at the general for direction, but his expression seemed to indicate that he didn't consider the princesses to be a threat.

The smaller blonde sister, who Monica understood to be Anastasia, called Stasi, turned to her next. "You're Monica?" Obviously Kirk had told the sisters about her, as Thad had instructed Alec.

"Yes." As Monica awkwardly wondered whether she should curtsy or shake the princess's hand, Stasi surprised her with a hug.

"Thank you for bringing my brother home." The petite princess squeezed her tight, followed by Isabelle, who embraced her and thanked her, as well.

Too dumbfounded to respond, Monica wondered if she should explain that Thad hadn't returned because of any winsome request on her part. Did anyone understand why Petrela stood among them? They seemed far too distracted by their brother's return to consider the question. But they'd learn the details soon enough. Besides, Monica wasn't entirely certain she could trust her voice, having often wondered how her sisters-in-law might receive her, but never envisioning them welcoming her so warmly.

Of course, once they learned she'd hidden their

nephew away for five years, only to have him kidnapped and used as a pawn in exchange for the crown they'd worked so hard to reclaim, they might feel quite differently.

"Where's Alexander?" Thad asked, looking around.

"He isn't doing very well on the stairs, or else he could have come down to greet you. He and his fiancée, Lily, are waiting upstairs in the conference room. We promised to join them the moment you arrived," Isabelle explained.

Thad absorbed the news with a nod. "Perhaps that's the best place to meet. We have twenty-seven hours." He sighed, seemingly unwilling to explain everything in the foyer, only to reexplain once they joined the others upstairs. "Shall we join them?"

Kirk led the way. "Levi Grenaldo and Dom Procopio are up there, as well."

Monica felt a sense of relief hearing that Dom Procopio would be joining them, the only other person who'd known she was married. Having kept the marriage a secret for so long, it would be a relief to be around someone who'd been there in the beginning.

She followed quietly up the stairs, letting Petrela and his men shadow Thaddeus closely, since they seemed so intent on doing so. Most of the others had entered the conference room by the time Monica came around the corner.

Dom Procopio waited just outside the conference

room. The round-eyed older man extended his arms toward her when he saw her, and she returned his embrace gladly. Finally, after so many new faces, someone familiar. Though the sight of the man who'd officiated at her wedding brought back bittersweet memories, she was grateful for the hug.

"Monica," he greeted her warmly. "It's good to see you. It's been too long."

Choked by emotion, Monica nodded and followed him into the room. They'd brought quite a crowd with them, including half a dozen of Petrela's men, besides the two he'd stationed outside the doors. But the room was quite large, and its vast space seemed to absorb the figures.

Nonetheless, the presence of Octavian's men had a stifling effect on Thad's siblings, who glanced at them repeatedly, as though beginning to question why the men were there. Thad's emotions also seemed stunted, though Monica wasn't sure whether to attribute that to Petrela and his men or the long-term freezing effects of his Arctic sojourn. The guards took their places around the periphery while Thad and his siblings made their way toward the table.

A man stepped forward and linked his arm around Princess Isabelle's waist. Just as she guessed who he was, he extended his hand to Thad and introduced himself.

"Levi Grenaldo." Isabelle's fiancé.

Thad shook his hand, recognition in his eyes. "You're a lawyer?"

"I specialize in international law."

Isabelle jumped in to add, "Levi's father, Nicolas, is the president of Sanctuary International, the asylum organization that was instrumental in getting me safely out of Lydia."

"Sanctuary International would be happy to continue to help Lydia in any way possible," Levi added. "Unfortunately, in the course of Isabelle's adventures, we discovered one of our trusted agents was secretly working for the conspirators who were targeting Isabelle."

"I appreciate all you've done." Thad thanked him. "I agree with your wisdom in keeping your father's organization out of the loop from this point on. We need to maintain secrecy as much as possible. I'll explain momentarily."

Monica ducked around the massive mahogany table that occupied the center of a room surrounded by wood inlaid walls interspersed with bookshelves. A marble fireplace dominated the far wall. The crackling blaze kept the damp chill of the stone palace at bay. She took a chair by the dancing flames, hoping to ward off some of the cold that had settled in her bones after her Arctic adventure. Even as she soaked up the warmth, she prayed that her son wasn't too cold or frightened.

The mere thought of him sent tears springing to

her eyes, and she bit her lip to hold them back, glancing up quickly to see if anyone had noticed.

But no one seemed to be paying her any attention. Thad's sisters had seemed to catch on to the nervous vibe—that this wasn't a happy homecoming at all. They exchanged questioning glances, and Stasi played nervously with her necklace.

Thad looked at Monica for just a moment, long enough for her to be certain he'd seen the tears that were about to fall. Then he looked away, his stony expression unreadable.

Monica let out a long, slow breath before inhaling again deeply. She had to keep her cool. She'd already put up with a long trek to Alaska as well as the flight to Lydia. It wouldn't do to lose it now—not when her son's future hung so precariously in the balance.

Thad turned to see his brother, Alexander, rising from his chair to greet him. After six long years, the soldier prince had changed greatly—even more so, given that Thad had seen little of him in the six years prior to that, when he'd gone off to the United States for school. Now, as Thad understood it, Alec had been appointed to the role of General of the Lydian Army, having defeated General David Bardici, one of the conspirators who'd been helping Octavian from inside that branch of the Lydian military.

Alec regarded him silently for a moment before

hobbling forward to embrace him. Growing up, they'd squabbled and fought constantly. But Alec had just risked his life to preserve a crown Thad wasn't sure he'd ever wear. Alec shuffled back a step on a walking boot, and Thad pointed to the orthopedic brace. "You were injured?"

"Shot in the foot." Alec pointed to the bright-eyed woman who'd been sitting next to him at the table. "By her uncle."

The woman rose. "I'm Lillian—"

"Bardici," Thad finished with her, remembering the name from Kirk's summary on the way to the palace.

"My fiancée." Alec wrapped an arm around the woman, who beamed up at him.

As the recently engaged couple gazed at each other happily, Thad glanced at Monica, who sat by the fire, her attention on the dancing flames as her chest rose and fell with slow, even breaths. He'd never had the opportunity to introduce her to his family as his fiancée. He'd never introduced her at all.

Suddenly a formal introduction felt long overdue.

He cleared his throat as he crossed the room to stand by her chair. "Thank you all for being here. I know you've made immense sacrifices to make this meeting possible, and I realize you're all eager to see the current situation stabilized. You've overcome many foes to bring us to this point, but there is one enemy who has yet to be defeated."

His siblings and their fiancés looked back at him, as did Dom Procopio, his father's most trusted spiritual advisor. But they also looked nervously at General Marc Petrela—a figure known to his siblings and, most likely, by extension, to their fiancés, as well. His presence clearly stifled their willingness to speak.

Even Petrela himself seemed to realize the difficulty his presence presented. To Thad's surprise, Petrela stepped around to his men and murmured something to each of them before escorting them to the door. He stayed in the room, but closed it behind the last of his men before turning to face the royal family. "Now you may speak freely," he announced.

Isabelle shook her head, looking back and forth between the general and Thad. "I—I don't understand what he's doing here."

"It's a long story," Thad told his sister. "And we don't have much time—"

"You haven't explained that, either," Stasi accused.

Thad closed his eyes, blocking out the sight of his family as he tried to think. After so many years of not feeling anything, being in the presence of Monica and his siblings all at once, on top of finding out he had a son…he was overwhelmed. He wasn't sure what kind of guidance he could give under the circumstances.

To his surprise, Monica picked up the line of discussion that he'd dropped, speaking the name the rest of them seemed so hesitant to utter. "Octavian, the man you know as '8,' has yet to be defeated."

"But is he still a real threat?" Stasi questioned. "He's never shown his face. Perhaps he's been scared away now that we've defeated so many of his henchmen."

"We haven't defeated them *all,*" Levi Grenaldo replied. Isabelle's fiancé had been sitting quietly at the table beside Isabelle. Now he dropped her hand to gesture. "Lydia had three generals, who Isabelle discovered were conspiring with Octavian. David Bardici, Corban Lucca and—" he turned an accusing look at the general "—Marc Petrela."

For one long moment everyone seemed to freeze. Thad fully expected Petrela to jump in and defend himself, to make an excuse for why he'd been included in the emails between the conspiring parties, but he said nothing.

Alec continued the story where Levi had left off. "David Bardici is dead, Corban Lucca was routed in Milan but we don't know what's become of him, and we don't know where Marc Petrela stands." The prince raised an eyebrow toward the general.

Petrela had been sitting silently near the far corner of the conference table ever since he'd dismissed his guards. Now he spoke so quietly that everyone had to strain to hear him. "I am glad to hear that the royal family is on top of the situation. I understand your hesitancy to accept my presence, given the inherent awkwardness of my recent associations."

Monica coughed derisively, but didn't say anything.

Thad understood the source of her consternation. Petrela had made their lives miserable for the past twenty hours. Why would he attempt to distance himself from Octavian using rhetoric?

And yet, as Petrela continued his explanation, Thad began to consider that the general's claims might have some credence.

"I grant that I have been involved with Octavian to a highly suspicious degree. I myself have frequently questioned what my own motives were, and who I think I'm working for. I've had my doubts whether I was doing the right thing, especially over the last two weeks. And yet, we now stand closer than ever before to overcoming this madman who has for so long had his sights set on overtaking Lydia."

"We?" Anastasia questioned. "Are you claiming to be one of us?"

"If Octavian asks, I will deny it," Petrela admitted openly. "But to you I will confess, I have been cooperating with Octavian only to gather evidence against him—to spy on him and, ultimately, to undo him. There is nothing I can say or do at this moment that will prove to you precisely where I stand, but I can promise you this—when the moment of truth comes, and it is fast approaching, then you will know I have always been on your side. Until then, you will just have to trust me."

While silence descended over the room, Thad considered Petrela's claims. Was he telling the truth? Thad couldn't think of a way to test him—not without wasting far more time than they had to waste.

Alexander shook his head. "I'm sorry. I don't know how I can trust you."

Petrela didn't appear to be fazed by the prince's statement. "It doesn't really matter. You have no choice."

SIX

The general looked at Thad. "Will you explain it to them?"

Thad felt as though all his strength had been drained, along with his ability to form a coherent sentence. Where should he begin? With the news that he had a son? With Octavian's demands for the scepter? He stood and crossed the room toward Monica. She'd made sense of his muddled thoughts earlier. There had been a time when she'd known him better than anyone and could supply the words he couldn't find on the tip of his tongue.

Could she do that again for him today? He hoped so, because he felt at a total loss.

As the warmth of the fire seeped into the cold of his bones, Thad stood next to Monica and tried to spell out all that was on the line. He didn't know if Octavian could be stopped—but he was quite sure he needed the help of his siblings if he was going to have any chance of keeping their kingdom out of Octavian's hands. "Octavian *has* acted. Not only is he a sincere threat, but as of this moment, he has the upper hand."

Thad let his hand settle onto Monica's shoulder, and he suddenly found it easier to speak. "Kirk, what have you told them about my wife?"

"Just that you have one, and her name is Monica."

Thad nodded. "Six years ago, I secretly married Monica Miller, only to learn days later about our father's entanglements with the man known by the code name 8. Octavian demanded that I sign away my claim to the throne that had been made legal when I was formally declared Father's successor following his coronation. At the same time, he wanted me to hand over the priceless relic of our family's reign, the Scepter of Charlemagne, which would solidify his claim to the throne."

"Thank God you didn't." Isabelle flashed him an appreciative smile.

Thaddeus wished he could smile back, but the sorrow inside him was too great to allow his mouth to turn upward with that expression. "I hid the scepter and went into hiding, abandoning my wife in hopes that she would never be discovered."

All eyes turned to Monica.

"Were you discovered?" Stasi asked in a small voice.

Monica looked up at him as though waiting for him to speak. Thad could hardly form the words. "Tell them," he whispered.

"I don't know when Octavian found me." Her voice sounded thick, weighed down with pain. "I've lived for six years in Seattle, near my parents. I finished my doctoral degree in ancient languages and started teaching. There was never anything that would have indicated that this madman realized I existed."

Kirk rubbed his face with his hands as she spoke, and shook his head as she finished. "You don't suppose, when I started to mention her over the phone…"

General Petrela's deep voice murmured. "Octavian didn't know about Monica until just a few days ago. Even then, he didn't have a name, just a possibility that there was a woman in Thad's past. He started looking into every woman Thad was known to have been friends with prior to his disappearance. That's how he tracked down Monica."

Kirk's face blanched pale. "It had to have been the phone call, then—or else it was when I explained to the family about Monica, right after the phone call. But there were just the six of us in the room then, so unless there's a mole, or a unless Octavian has some way of listening in—"

"Don't forget," Petrela cautioned them, "Octavian had control of this very palace for almost a full week following the ambush. I wasn't in the area, but I know he sent instructions to Viktor Bosch to make modifications. Devices were sent—but I don't know what they were, and Viktor is dead, so he can't tell us."

"Listening devices?" Isabelle shuddered. "Do you think he has the whole palace bugged?"

"This palace has over a hundred rooms." Thad recalled that Viktor Bosch had been the head of the royal guard at the time of the ambush on the motorcade. He leveled a look at the general. "Does Octavian have the manpower to monitor that many devices at once?"

"He does," Petrela confirmed, "though I understand the shipment contained only two devices. I can't say for certain what the devices were or where we might find them. They could have been any number of things. Given the time constraints I advise you to carry on as though you can't be heard."

Anastasia gave a little whimper, and Thad realized he'd brought his family nothing but bad news and dreadful uncertainties. They'd been so hopeful that he might help them end their ordeal. And they had yet to hear the worst part.

There wasn't anything to be gained by letting the possibility of devices distract them from their discussion. Thad had no intention of revealing anything that Octavian didn't already know. But they needed to press on—the clock was ticking.

Thad took a deep breath. "I'm indebted to you, Kirk, for all the sacrifices you've made on behalf of Lydia. You saved Stasi's life, you went on trial for my murder, you kept my secrets for six years."

A sniffling sound caught Thad's attention, and he looked down to see Monica fighting back tears.

Thad finished quickly. "I won't blame you for what happened. Whatever Octavian may have heard, however he overheard it, somehow that led Octavian to my wife. And not just to *her*." He swallowed, and met the eyes of everyone else in the room before finding the strength to finish his statement. "Unbeknownst to me, during our brief marriage, Monica conceived a son. His name is Peter.

"Yesterday, he was kidnapped from his grandparents' house. Octavian is holding him prisoner. If I don't hand over the scepter and sign over the crown at noon tomorrow, Octavian has vowed to kill him."

Monica couldn't stand it any longer. She'd promised herself she wouldn't get emotional, but the stark summary of Peter's predicament sent silent tears streaming down her cheeks. She rose to excuse herself from the room.

Before she could navigate her way around the long table, Thad stepped in front of her. She looked up at him to apologize. He wrapped his strong arms around her shoulders and held her against his chest.

The tears flowed freely then, too much emotion and confusion fueling them. She'd failed her son. Octavian had him—and from what she'd heard,

Octavian had every advantage over them. Would she ever see Peter again? Even if she did, would Octavian have taught him lies and corrupted his tender heart?

Thad supported her, holding her up when she felt like sagging to the ground. After the formal distance he'd kept between them, she was surprised to feel his fingers lightly rubbing her back in the soothing manner that had brought her comfort years before. But back then, he'd been easing the sting of a harsh test grade and the loss of her cat.

The world had gotten so much more complicated since then, and she hadn't realized how much she'd missed his touch. Or maybe she had, but she'd been so angry with him, she was unwilling to admit to herself how much she missed him.

Thad's announcement had silenced the room, and it felt as though too many precious minutes crept by before anyone spoke.

"I'm sorry," Kirk said finally. "I'm so sorry. I never dreamed—"

"We can't go back in time and undo what's happened." Thad's voice rumbled in her ear. "We have until noon on Saturday to sort it out."

Sniffling back her tears, Monica realized the smell of oil that had clung to him so strongly had begun to dissipate. In its place, she breathed in the old familiar scent of her husband, evoking memories she'd refused to think about since he'd left her.

But now he was here, holding her, and she felt her wounded heart giving a little groan.

"But, Thaddeus—" Stasi's plea prompted Monica to peek out past the safe haven of Thad's arms "—what can we do? We've got to get your little boy away from that horrid man."

"He's not just a little boy," Isabelle corrected her sister. "He's a prince. Let's not forget the reason our lives have been spared over the course of this ordeal. At various times and in various ways, Octavian considered each of us a potential avenue to power. He tried to marry me off to a puppet mogul in hopes of producing an heir. *That* plan would have taken months, even years to come to fruition, and now he's holding a descendent of Lydia prisoner?"

Levi picked up on his fiancée's line of reasoning. "I doubt Octavian has any intention of letting Peter go free, even if we hand over the scepter. He's far too useful to him."

"Worse than that." Thad articulated the scenario he'd suggested to Monica earlier. "If we hand over the scepter, we render ourselves obsolete."

Alec huffed. "Worse than obsolete. We'd be the biggest threat to his power."

"That wicked little tyrant." Stasi pounded her petite fist against the table. "He's dreamed for years of knocking us all off. If we give him what he wants, he'll kill us just to ease his frustration." She stared at her oldest brother. "You *can't* play into his plans. It won't help anything."

"And yet—" Lillian Bardici cleared her throat "—we've got to rescue that little boy. Kidnapping is a crime. Can't we ask Interpol to help?"

Levi, the international law expert, shook his head. "The International Police Organization can't interfere in political matters. They've got to maintain their neutrality. I'm afraid they'd only turn us down."

"I've been working with the United Nations peacekeeping team that was dispatched in the wake of the ambush," Isabelle added. "They strictly avoid any actions that could be interpreted as taking sides. In the eyes of the world, this is a political issue. We can point to all the crimes Octavian has committed, but Octavian claims he's been wronged, as well—that Father has reneged on the agreements between them."

"What about the emails you intercepted?" Stasi questioned her sister. "Don't they prove Octavian was conspiring with Lydia's generals?"

"Unfortunately—" Isabelle blew out a frustrated breath "—I was able to retrieve only one week's worth of emails. Yes, it tells us there was a conspiracy, but we don't know how the plots *began*. Petrela claims he was only part of the plot because he wanted to stop Octavian." She pointed to the general. "Any of the others could make the same claim, and we have no way of proving otherwise. You can't arrest someone for receiving an email."

Alec nodded in agreement with his sister's analysis. "There's a chance one or more of the generals may have been acting to defend the crown—receiving the emails as a way of keeping tabs on Octavian for us, just as Petrela claims he's been doing." Alec's tone, along with the sideways glance he shot the general, betrayed his underlying reluctance to believe Petrela's claims.

"In that case, they should have been reporting back to the crown," Isabelle noted.

"They may have been," Thad acknowledged. "Father is in no position to tell us either way."

Lily cleared her throat. "It could take a long time to sort out everyone's guilt and innocence. We've got just over a day left to rescue Peter. Let's not let ourselves get so distracted that we lose sight of that."

Alec took his fiancée's hand. "I agree. Peter must be liberated and returned to his mother. But how are we going to accomplish that?"

Monica felt another wave of silent tears rising up as those around the table pledged their intention to free her son. Thad's arms shifted around her, and she realized she'd gotten so caught up in the conversation, she'd forgotten how inappropriate it was for her to be so close to him. It felt so right to be in his arms again. She almost wished she could stay there, but instead she stepped away. After all, she was still angry with him for his role in her son's capture. She'd spent the past six years resenting him for leaving her. She wasn't ready to forget that—certainly not as long as a madman had her son.

She swallowed back her tears as the team members struggled to find a solution to Peter's predicament.

"Let's not forget who we're dealing with," Levi reminded everyone. "Whenever we've underestimated Octavian, he's always turned out to be two steps ahead of us. Thad, you've said he lacks two things to accomplish his plans—your signature and the Scepter of Charlemagne."

Monica looked at Levi for a long moment, wondering, as she assumed everyone else was wondering, what he was getting at.

Levi looked around the room slowly before asking, "Do we know for certain he doesn't already have the scepter?"

A shot of fear sizzled through her, enough to compel her to back farther away from Thad and blink up at him. He'd been the last person among them to touch the scepter, but that had been six years before.

Everyone looked to the general.

"Octavian kept many secrets from me," Petrela acknowledged. "I couldn't probe too deeply in matters beyond my jurisdiction for fear of attracting attention to myself. I'll tell you anything I know that might help you, but I really can't say whether he has the scepter. Octavian holds his cards very close to his chest."

Thad shook his head slowly. "Then we don't know."

"Levi raises an excellent point," Dom Procopio said, speaking up for the first time. "If you only have one advantage against this Octavian fellow, you ought to be certain you really have it. Otherwise you're playing with nothing, and you're bound to walk into a trap."

A murmur of agreement passed through the siblings, but Kirk balked at the idea. "Monica was safe for six years until I spoke of her," he reminded them. "If the scepter has been safely hidden away for that long, I'm loath to uncover it now, not when Octavian's bound to have spies and moles everywhere." He shot a wary look at Petrela. "I'd hate to lose it simply because we were afraid to trust its hiding place."

Thad took a step closer to the head of the table and placed his fists on the glossy surface of the wood, leaning down slightly to meet everyone's eyes. "What do you think? I've heard both sides of the argument, and they both have valid points. Shall I uncover the scepter or keep it hidden?"

"I think we need to pray about it before we make that decision." Isabelle locked hands with Levi on one side of her, and Stasi on the other.

"Yes, let's pray," Alec agreed, bowing his head as his fingers clasped Lillian's hand on one side, and drew Dom Procopio's on the other. "Will you lead the prayer, Deacon?"

As the others clasped hands and bowed their heads around the table, Monica felt Thad's frustration simmering beside her. She stepped forward to take Thad's hand, but he turned away and faced the fire, his arms crossed firmly.

The others hadn't noticed. Their heads were bowed and their eyes closed as Monica stretched to close the gap between General Petrela and Dom, who'd already opened the prayer.

The siblings around the table joined in, thanking God for keeping them all safe and for bringing love into their lives. They prayed for healing for their father, and begged God to especially watch over Peter, before asking God's guidance about whether to look for the scepter.

Thaddeus spun around and faced them all from the head of the table the moment they said "Amen." Monica couldn't be sure if any of them had realized he wasn't praying with them, but his refusal to join them in prayer prickled at her. At the very least, he could have held hands and bowed his head along with them, even if he didn't believe God was listening. If he hadn't thought God was there, it shouldn't have made any difference if he participated in the prayer.

No, it was almost as though he was angry at God, rather than unbelieving.

Before she could consider the issue, Thad cleared his throat. "It seems to me the risks of fetching the scepter are outweighed by the benefits. We need it by tomorrow anyway, so there's no sense putting off going after it. But in order to reduce the odds of detection, I'll retrieve it by myself."

"Right now?" Alec asked.

"I'll wait until dark. Right now, I strongly feel I ought to visit our mother. She's at Father's bedside at the hospital?" Thad seemed to be in a hurry to end the meeting. Monica wondered if the prayer had made him that uncomfortable.

"Yes. I can take you there," Stasi offered.

"I'd appreciate that. I'll freshen up and change clothes first. Can I meet you in the foyer?" He shot a glance at Petrela, as though challenging him to try and stop him, or to tie him up like an animal again.

The general simply winked.

Monica couldn't help but wonder whose side the man was really on. Could they trust him? Did they have any choice? With just shy of a day remaining before Octavian expected the scepter, they had to focus on the mission before them—and just be grateful Petrela was letting them go about their business unfettered.

Thad and Stasi set a time, and then Isabelle offered to take Monica to the suite that had been prepared for her. Monica thanked her and followed, making note of the time Thad had planned to meet

Stasi for the trip to the hospital. He hadn't invited her, but she still hoped to tag along. She'd never been introduced to her mother-in-law, and if there was any chance Thad was planning to break the news to Queen Elaine that she had a grandson, Monica wanted to be there.

Thad wasn't surprised to see Monica already waiting in the foyer as he made his way across the second-floor hall toward the stairs. She'd obviously taken advantage of the opportunity to freshen up and had her shoulder-length hair pulled up in front, draping down in back with thick curls that caught the light of the crystals from the chandelier above. Sunlight splashed across her as she turned to face him, and he saw that the blouse she wore, which had looked plain from the back, had a wide-collared neckline and a tie belt, accentuating her hourglass figure.

He nearly missed the next step, but he caught himself with his hand on the rail, and recovered fully by the time he reached her level. "You look—" He stopped himself before he could compliment her. Was it playing into Octavian's plans to admit the woman who'd caught his eye years before could still turn his head? He wanted to carry her off and make up for the long years they'd been apart. But Monica had made it clear that she was angry with him. Hopelessness clung to his soul.

"—refreshed," he finished.

The bright smile that had leaped to her lips when he started the sentence faded quickly at his disappointing words. Guilt stabbed him. She looked far more than refreshed. She was the embodiment of his every dream, the balm for his hurting soul, the paradise at the end of his long journey. And if he intended to defeat Octavian, she was absolutely off-limits.

Thad swallowed back the guilty feeling. It didn't matter. He had a job to do.

"Any sign of the general?"

"He was talking to his guards earlier—my impression was that he was instructing them to give us a longer leash, so to speak. And I hope he's asked them not to report to Octavian directly."

"That would be a relief. What do you think of his claim that he's really on our side?" Thad met Monica's eyes, intending only to gauge what she thought of the general. But when she looked up at him through her thick eyelashes, he felt his hardened heart swell with longing, and he was tempted to pull her into his arms again, to feel the press of her lips against his.

But that would be foolishness.

"I'd love to believe him, but it sounds too good to be true, don't you think? Besides, if he's been working on our side, he could have mentioned it sooner. It sounds too convenient to me."

Thad nodded. Her ideas aligned with his. "He knows he's outnumbered. He's made a handy excuse. I won't challenge him as long as he's willing to let us move about freely—but I won't trust him, either."

Footsteps pattered above them and he turned, expecting Stasi, in time to see Isabelle instead.

"Oh, good, I caught you in time." Isabelle hurried down the stairs. "You can't go out the front door."

"Why not?" Thad felt miffed at her suggestion. He barely had a day left—he didn't want to waste single minute with foolishness. "It's the most direct route."

"That's the door the paparazzi tend to monitor. We're very fortunate they haven't gotten wind of your return already. The last thing we need is a media frenzy to deal with."

Thad realized what his sister was suggesting. As a popular princess, Isabelle had long been plagued by the media, and she had understood them as well as anyone. "We'll have to sneak out the back way."

Isabelle agreed. "We should be able to dodge them while you're here, since they aren't expecting you and most of them assume you're long dead. But eventually, we'll have to hold a press conference and announce your return."

"Not until this mess with Octavian is sorted out." For all Thad knew, he'd end up in hiding once again—and it would be a thousand times simpler to hide if no one realized he'd ever returned.

"Of course, not until then. We don't have time to

deal with it right now. There's Stasi." She nodded at her sister, who was entering on Kirk's arm.

"Thanks, Isabelle." Thad turned and offered her a small smile—the most he could manage after so many years out of the practice.

"No problem. Get my nephew back." His sister winked.

Thad hurried to keep up with Stasi, who had Monica by the arm, and rattled off the names of rooms as though she was leading a whirlwind tour. "The north dining room has secret passages leading to the kitchen and the garden."

"You don't need to tell her about the secret passages," Thad chided his little sister. "That knowledge is privy only to the royal family."

"She's part of the royal family," Stasi challenged him.

Thad wanted to disagree with her on that point, but he couldn't think of a valid argument. They quickly reached the back exit, where Kirk and Stasi trotted over to the royal garages.

"Do we need to call a driver?" Thad noticed all the keys were locked in a glass cabinet.

"I've got it." Kirk pressed his thumb against the touch pad and pulled out a set of keys. "We don't want to draw any attention to ourselves." He led them to a black Ford Focus, which Thad had noticed earlier was one of the most ubiquitous cars on the Lydian streets. "Hop in."

Thad circled around to the front passenger's side, but Stasi cut him off.

"I don't think so. The missing monarch is not allowed to sit in the front seat where anyone might see him. That's why we have tinted windows in back." She opened the rear door and gestured for him to climb in.

Thad squeezed his large frame into the compact backseat. He tried not to notice how close he was to Monica or the way their fingers tangled as they searched for the clasps to their seat belts. He tried not to think about the bare spot on her ring finger where she'd once worn his wedding band. But being back in Lydia and being close to her made it impossible to fight the joy he felt marrying her.

Fortunately, he didn't have long to think about the distracting proximity to his wife. A moment after Kirk zipped through the back gates, two cars emerged from near the bushes and took to the street directly behind them. Thad caught just a glimpse of one leering driver before the glare of the sun blocked his view.

He instinctively ducked down and met Monica's eyes as she did the same.

"That looked like one of the guards from the plane," she whispered. "And General Petrela in the passenger's seat. I thought he was going to leave us alone."

"Perhaps he only wanted to make us *think* they

were leaving us alone," Thad growled with displeasure, redoubling his doubts about the general's claims. "If they steal the scepter out from under me the moment I uncover it for them, they won't have to give up Peter."

"Do you want me to try to lose them?" Kirk asked.

"I don't see the point. Petrela knows we're heading to the hospital to see Mom."

"I'd hate for Petrela to tell Octavian we're not cooperating," Monica agreed. She leaned toward him, her mouth open partway, her eyes intent.

Time seemed to slow as her face drew nearer to his. He could imagine his lips closing over hers as they had so many times before, so many years before. It would be all too easy to wrap his arms around her and hold her close, until he was willing to give up everything for her, including his kingdom.

And that was precisely what Octavian wanted.

Thad started to lean away from her, but Monica tipped his chin toward her and studied him, scowling. "Isabelle had an excellent point. Paparazzi or not, we don't want anyone at the hospital recognizing you. You've got enough of a prickly five-o'clock shadow to obscure the outline of your jaw," she surmised. "And your hair is much longer than it ever was." She turned her attention to the front seat. "Kirk, can Thad borrow your cap and sunglasses?"

"Gladly." He slipped them to Stasi, keeping one hand on the wheel. The little princess handed them back, watching with interest as her brother slipped them on.

"There." Stasi smiled triumphantly "*I* hardly recognize you. And since everyone else still thinks you're dead, no one should be expecting to see you."

"Good." Thad exhaled a breath he hadn't realized he'd been holding. "Let's visit Mom while we've got the chance." He didn't voice the rest of his thoughts out loud. He didn't figure anyone needed the reminder, especially not after the appearance of Octavian's men. They had their work cut out for them if they were going to get Peter back, and the clock was ticking.

SEVEN

Monica felt her heart beating in her throat as they made their way through the antiseptic halls of the hospital, trailing Stasi on what must have been a well-worn route to King Philip's room, past posted layers of security.

Her fear didn't come from the general or his guards who trailed them down the hall but from the anticipation of meeting the queen for the first time. They left Petrela and his men next to the security guards who held vigil over the isolated wing where the king lay. Monica hung back in the doorway while Stasi entered first, planting a kiss on her mother's cheeks and her father's forehead before stepping back for Kirk to greet Queen Elaine.

Kirk entered after Stasi, with Thad trailing his childhood best friend, lingering just out of his mother's range of sight behind the privacy curtain that shielded the hospital bed from the door.

From her vantage point just inside the doorway, Monica could see all of them, though they couldn't all see one another. Thad glanced at her, and she gave him an encouraging smile.

Meanwhile, Kirk had kissed the air next to his future mother-in-law's pale face and cleared his throat. "We brought you a visitor."

Elaine glanced at Monica in the doorway, and shook her head. "No visitors. Only family. He hasn't had a good day."

As the queen looked to the fallen king, Monica realized for the first time how deathly pale the recently dethroned monarch's face looked under the ventilator and how little the sheets over his chest rose and fell. She pinched her eyes shut, praying that he would recover. Praying that somehow, someday, he'd get to meet the grandson he didn't even know he had.

"They are family," Kirk murmured, reaching back to open the curtain.

Monica watched the confusion on the queen's face change to disbelief and joy.

Thad peeled off the cap and sunglasses as he stepped toward his mother, who nearly melted into her chair before rising, shakily, to her feet. Thad gathered her up into his arms.

"My baby." Elaine patted his shoulder, her cheeks streaming with tears she had likely given up all hope of ever crying. "You're here. You're really here."

Even Thad's eyes glimmered wet as he held his mother. He didn't try to speak. There was too much to be said, and Monica couldn't imagine where he would even begin.

Monica felt fat tears dripping down her cheeks, spilling off the tip of her nose, but there was little she could do to stop them. God was good. He had united this mother with her son.

Surely He would unite her with Peter again, too.

Somehow.

"You came back? Are you going to take the throne?" The queen pulled away from her son just far enough to look up into his face.

Sorrow warred with the joy of reunion as Thad's lips twitched. Monica could feel his struggle to answer his mother's question. In fact, Monica had begun to wonder, given the things Thad had said of late, whether he had any hope of being crowned king.

So she was very relieved to hear him answer. "I'm going to try."

After a good deal of hugging and beaming, Stasi handed her mom some tissues before she and Kirk snuck away, promising to wait down the hall for the two of them.

It wasn't until Kirk and Stasi had left the room that Elaine seemed to notice Monica. "And who is this?"

"I'd like to introduce you to Monica Miller." Thad gestured for her to come forward.

She had to will her feet to move. Thad had embraced all his family members, demonstrating genuine affection toward them, but he'd only ever held her that one time in the conference room, and she'd decided since then the gesture had simply been a symbolic act, to put on a united front before his siblings. The rest of the time he kept her at arm's length, which she figured was probably a wise move, since she might have slugged him out of repressed resentment if he got within range.

Now she crept forward trepidatiously. The queen blinked at her, dabbing her cheeks with tissues, waiting for Thad to explain further.

Monica wondered what he would say. Would he claim her as his wife?

"Monica is—" Thad spoke slowly, buying time as he chose his words "—the mother of my son."

"You have a son?"

It was all Monica could do to nod, as Thad's distancing words squeezed her heart.

"Well, where is he?" Elaine looked past them, as though Peter might be hiding shyly just beyond the curtain.

"He's, um, well—" Thad cleared his throat. "Octavian has him."

"Octavian?" Elaine seemed to flutter back down into her chair, her face even paler than before.

The tears, which Monica realized she'd never wiped from her face, now poured down freely again.

This wasn't how she'd ever envisioned being introduced to the queen. Not nearly.

Thad took the chair next to his mother's, holding her hand as he went back in time and explained all that had happened, dismissing his relationship with Monica by using the word *eloped*. Not once did he call her his wife. Not once did he state that they'd been in love.

Slowly, Monica crept back to the doorway, until she was able to lean back against the solid support of the wall and watch her husband with his mother as though it was a scene on a screen and not something that touched the deepest parts of her heart.

At least Queen Elaine's face softened when Thad showed her the pictures of Peter Monica had passed to him on Octavian's plane. But her expression grew stiff when she glanced back up at Monica, and she shook her head as though surely there had been a mistake.

Finally, Thad sat back in his chair, finished with his tale.

The queen seemed to be having trouble swallowing.

"Can I get you something, Mother?" Thad asked.

"Yes, please." She pulled a few coins from her purse. "There's a beverage machine down the hall." She told him where to find it and what drink she preferred.

As he stepped past her, Monica thought about

going with him, but Queen Elaine patted the chair Thad had vacated and spoke three words that sent a fearful chill down her spine. "Monica? Let's chat."

Monica wished she'd bolted out the door after Thaddeus while she had the chance. More than that, she wished she'd bolted at the first sight of him years before. But there was nothing for it now but to cross the room under the queen's scrutinizing gaze and sit as primly as possible in the chair next to hers.

"Are you still married to my son?" Queen Elaine must have realized Thad wouldn't be gone long. She certainly wasn't wasting any time with small talk.

"Yes."

"You don't act married."

"We haven't seen each other in six years." Monica was fairly certain Thad had already expressed that part of the story, but it was the only explanation she could give.

"You're upset with him."

"He left me." Monica felt the need to defend herself from what felt like a full-blown attack. "And now my son is in the hands of that awful Octavian." She didn't add the part about their slim chances of getting Peter back. The queen had enough on her mind, what with Philip in a coma and her family having been attacked.

"It will all come out all right." Elaine patted her hand where she gripped the arm rest of her chair. "Have a little faith."

Monica coughed back her reaction to the queen's patronizing statement. She knew the woman was only trying to help and was under grave stress herself. Still, it struck Monica as ironic that after all the prayers she'd prayed, and after Thad's refusal to pray, his mother would tell *her* to have faith.

Elaine seemed to feel the need to reassure her. "Thad will get his son back. He trusts God—"

"No, he doesn't," Monica burst out, in spite of her efforts to hold back.

The older woman studied her carefully a moment. "He doesn't? He always did."

"I know he did. He encouraged me in my faith considerably during college. But now he won't even pray with his siblings. He scoffed at the suggestion when I tried to get him to pray with me." Monica lowered her voice, realized Thad could return at any moment. "I'm afraid he's lost his faith during his time in exile. Not that I blame him, having been there, but this is the worst possible time for him to be adrift."

The queen had her hand, and now squeezed it reassuringly. "He needs God's help now more than ever. I'll keep you both in my prayers. And little Peter, too."

"Thank you." For a long moment, Monica looked at her shoes and listened silently to the constant beeps and ticks of the machines that monitored King Philip's vital signs.

Then Thad reappeared with the queen's beverage, and she took a drink before reaching out and grasping her son's hand.

Elaine raised a knowing eyebrow at Monica before suggesting, "We should pray before you leave."

But Thad immediately shook his head. "I'm sorry. We've got a lot of ground to cover, Mother." He shot Monica a conspiratorial look. "Our *guest* in the hallway wants us to get going."

"Then we should be going," Monica agreed, realizing that General Petrela's wishes were to be obeyed above everyone else's—she didn't want him reporting back that they weren't cooperating. She didn't want to give Octavian any excuse to hurt her son.

Thad felt guilty leaving his parents so abruptly, but the general had caught him when he'd gone to fetch his mother's beverage, and delivered an urgent message.

Octavian wasn't happy.

And that wasn't good. Thad led the general and Monica to the waiting room down the hall where Kirk and Stasi were holed up.

"What does he want?" Thad growled at the general as soon as he had the door closed behind them. "I have until noon tomorrow to hand over the scepter."

"He asked where we'd gone," Petrela began.

"And you told him?" Stasi squeaked.

The general's stoic expression didn't falter. "He has ways of knowing where a person is. I've never quite pinpointed *how* he knows, but he knows. There's no point lying to him. I've seen what he does to men who claim to be other than where he knows them to be."

The solemn warning doused Thad's frustration at the general's interruption. The man wasn't playing games. If he was on their side, it had been more than kind of him to warn them. And if he wasn't on their side—well, the threat had teeth behind it.

Petrela continued. "He wants his representative to be allowed to visit your father."

"Under no circumstances—" Kirk began.

"Who's the representative?" Thad asked.

Petrela's mouth twitched.

"Tell us," Monica requested in that tone Thad had heard her use—the one that expected compliance.

"Corban Lucca."

"No!" Stasi leaped from the chair she'd been sitting in. "Lucca is the one who stole Father away to Milan, using the ambush as cover so everyone would think the king had deserted his country in its hour of need. Lucca was going to hand *me* over to Octavian's associates. We can't trust him."

"We can't trust Octavian, either," Monica agreed, "but he has my son, so I don't see how we can refuse him."

Kirk held up his hands, silencing them both. "I

spoke with some of the royal guards who are stationed in the hall. They said Lucca has already tried to use his authority as a Lydian general to get in to visit your father."

"Lucca should have been arrested on sight," Thad protested.

"I agree," Kirk acknowledged, "but the entire kingdom has been in upheaval. We need a king on the throne to restore order and see that all those who've conspired against the crown are brought to justice."

Thad ignored his friend's obvious insinuation. "They didn't let him past, at least?"

"Of course not. But apparently Lucca has been conferring with your father's doctor, as well. I was going to try to track down the doctor and find out what Lucca said."

"There's no time," Petrela cut in. "Octavian said he would send Lucca by immediately. I think you should move your father."

"But he's in a coma," Stasi protested. "His condition is fragile."

Thad studied the general. Was the man really trying to help them? Or was he counting on the move being too hard on the king's already-precarious condition?

Or was he stalling, keeping them distracted behind closed doors down the hall so Lucca could make his move? And why did Lucca want to see the king, anyway? Nothing good could possibly come of it.

Monica's thoughts must have followed the same trail, because she scooped up his hand and met his eyes. "I think we need to get back to your father's room right now."

Thad nodded. "Petrela, see if you can't track down that doctor, and while you're at it, find out if we can move my father to a different room. Stasi, call Alec. Let him know what's up." As he spoke, Thad backed toward the door, Monica's hand still tight in his. "Kirk, talk to the new head of the royal guard. Tell him we need more men stationed at the hospital right away."

"Yes, Your Highness," Kirk answered with a glimmer in his eye that reminded him of his friend's suggestion that he take the crown.

Thad realized he *was* taking charge—but somebody had to. If Lucca was on his way, they needed to act, not sit around and try to reach a consensus. He hurried down the hallway toward his father's room.

"Can I borrow your phone?" Monica asked as they zipped past the guards.

"Sure. Why do you need it?"

"My father is a doctor. He might be able to advise us on how much damage moving your father might cause."

"Good idea." Thad handed her the phone while scanning the hallway. So far there was no sign of

Lucca, the Lydian general who was still technically the head of the Lydian Navy, though of course his involvement with the email conspiracy Isabelle had uncovered, combined with his other activities against the royal family, left him on the brink of court-martial.

When Thad ducked into his father's room, his mother rose quickly.

"I'm so glad you came back." She hugged him tight. "I was thinking about what you told me, about your son, Peter."

"Yes?"

"The entire time Corban Lucca held us hostage in Milan, he made clear the only reason we were still alive was because we were useful to him on his quest for the crown. But if he has your son—"

Monica stepped into the room, and the queen let the warning in her message linger in the air, unspoken.

"No answer." Monica shook her head as she returned his phone to him.

"I suppose they're on another line," Thad observed.

"I don't think so." Monica scowled. "It should have continued to ring, then. They have call waiting. But both of my parents' cell phones went straight to voice mail."

"Why would they have their phones turned off?" Thad asked. If they were hoping for news about their grandson, Monica's parents should have been waiting for the phone to ring.

Monica hugged herself. "I don't like it."

Thad pulled her by the shoulder into his embrace, his mother tucked under one arm, his wife under the other. The long-numb parts of his heart burned with the irony. Their embrace should have been a happy reunion.

Instead, his mind latched on to his mother's unspoken warning. Was Corban Lucca even now headed for them, ready to finish the job he'd been itching to complete since the moment the ambush had struck? Had his father become more of a liability than an asset?

"Monica, I'd like you to take my mother down the hall. There's a chapel just past the elevators—"

"I'm not leaving your father's bedside." The queen shuffled back to the chair where she'd been keeping silent vigil over her husband.

Thad pulled in a breath and tried to think how to impress upon his mother the importance of leaving for her own safety—without upsetting her further.

But the sound of shouting that carried from down the hall told him that he didn't have time to argue. He looked outside the door in time to see some of Petrela's guards, followed by more men who he didn't recognize and behind them all, a very determined-looking General Corban Lucca.

"Stop him!" Kirk's voice carried above the rustle of men and boots.

Thad looked down the other end of the hall, then back to his mother and Monica.

"Is there another way out?" Monica asked.

"There's a fire exit at the end of the hallway," the queen noted.

But Thad could see that Petrela and Lucca's men combined outnumbered the guards posted in the halls. He could see no sign of Petrela, nor of Kirk or Stasi. But as the newcomers held their guns on the men stationed along the corridor, Lucca made his way quickly toward the king's room.

"There's no time," Thad realized. Lucca could be inside the room in a matter of seconds. And while the men in the hallway were all packing weapons, Thad realized, too late, that he should have brought a gun. "Hide!" Thad pulled the privacy curtain closed, obscuring the king's bed. Then he stepped into the hallway to face Lucca.

General Corban Lucca of the Lydian Navy stopped just short of the doorway, flanked on either side by his men. He wasn't in uniform, but Thad quickly noted the bulge under the man's jacket.

He was packing heat.

So were the guards in the hallway, but Lucca's men had their weapons drawn, holding the guards at an impasse. Thad suddenly felt vulnerable, unarmed and caught slightly off guard.

Lucca spoke. "I appreciate your willingness to let me visit. I have been eager to pay my respects to our fallen monarch, but have been unable to get past the guards without your cooperation."

Thaddeus chafed at the general's words. His father wasn't fallen—that would imply he'd died. "I'm not allowing you to visit." He crossed his arms over his chest, more than aware that he wasn't wearing any sort of body armor. If Lucca decided to pull his weapon, Thad's only shot at survival would be to dive out of the way.

And leave a clear path to his father's bed.

"Step away, boy," Lucca challenged him.

Thad planted his feet firmly in the doorway. "I'm sorry if you were misled by your ease in getting this far. I'm not allowing you through to see my father." He cast a furtive glance down the hall, where he spotted Petrela easing himself past the posted men. What was the general up to? Was he working with Lucca? Would the two men pounce, overwhelming him the moment Petrela advanced past the guards?

Or could the general really be trusted?

Lucca followed the dart of his eyes, and smiled when he spotted Petrela's advancing figure. He turned his attention back to Thad. "Let me in, boy, before I have you removed."

"That won't be possible." Thad stood his ground. "You're the one who's going to be removed."

"Oh?" Lucca chuckled.

Thad felt his heartbeat thudding in his chest. He could hear rustling in the room behind him, and was more than aware of the precariousness of his situation. He wasn't just guarding his father. He was guarding his mother and wife, as well. For security reasons, his father had an interior suite—the room didn't even have a window. Other than a tiny closet of a bathroom, there was nothing inside the room but the bed, the medical equipment and a few chairs.

A few shots could fell them all, and with them the kingdom.

Thad had no choice but to keep Lucca talking—anything to delay him from drawing his weapon. Perhaps, if he kept him talking long enough, reinforcements would arrive. "General Corban Lucca, I'm afraid I'm going to have to have you taken into custody. We have evidence that you've been conspiring with Octavian to overthrow the monarchy. All of Octavian's conspirators are guilty of treason."

Lucca's laughter drowned out the last of his words. "Are you threatening me? Do you honestly think you're going to triumph over *Octavian?*" His obnoxious laughter echoed through the corridor. "If you want my advice, run away now." He gestured toward the emergency exit down the hall. "If you hurry, I'll let you escape alive for now."

"I won't leave—" Thad began, but Lucca immediately cut him off, getting in his face.

"Go back and hide at the edge of the earth. Maybe

Octavian will turn a blind eye to you once he has what he wants. *I'll* be rewarded handsomely for helping him. But as for your father, your allegiance is pitifully misplaced. I have the former king in my pocket. I've controlled him ever since the ambush, and I control him now. He's not going to wake up. He'll die in that bed."

Lucca took a step forward.

Thad didn't budge, but shot a quick glance at Petrela, who'd passed the last of the guards and was now within arm's reach of them both. What was he up to?

Returning his attention to Lucca, he watched as the man pivoted slightly to one side. His arm flicked back toward the bulge under his jacket.

At the same moment, Petrela flew into action.

"Get down!" Thad shouted into the room, unsure where his mother or Monica might be on the other side of the curtain. Thad lunged for Lucca's arm, but he already had his hand on the gun.

Lucca swung the gun high above his head, and Petrela reached for it, shouting at Thad, "Cover the women! I'd like to take him alive, if I can!"

With no time to ponder Petrela's intent, Thad stepped to the side of the doorway, out of the line of fire if the gun went off. Past the veiling drape of the curtain, he took in the entire room with one glance. His father lay still in the bed, but he couldn't see Monica or his mother anywhere.

His heart squeezed. Where had they hidden? It didn't matter—as long as they were safe.

Petrela stumbled back into the room, still grappling with Lucca over the gun. To Thad's relief, the men in the hallway appeared to be too confused by the scrabbling generals to act. They'd been given no order, so they stood still, watching the struggle with wide eyes.

Lucca lunged toward the room, but with the advantage of his height, Marc Petrela was able to get one hand on the barrel, pointing it toward the floor. Lucca strained against him, his finger dangerously close to the trigger as he struggled to point the muzzle toward the king lying helplessly in the hospital bed.

"Apprehend him!" Petrela called to the men frozen in the hallway.

A look of panic hit Lucca's eyes at the sound of the general's shout. Just as Thad realized the man had no intention of being subdued without getting a shot off, the man's finger stretched upward, compressing the trigger in a wild shot, as though he no longer cared where the gun was pointed.

The blast shattered the silence, and Thad ducked a moment too late, then staggered back, dazed, looking down at the spreading pool of blood on the floor.

EIGHT

Monica crouched beside Queen Elaine in the tiny bathroom, praying fervently that God would protect them from whatever was happening on the other side of the door. When a shot rang out, they both started and looked at each other in terrified fear, listening carefully for some sound that would indicate what had happened.

With visions of an injured Thad tearing through her thoughts, Monica had no choice but to reach for the doorknob. She had to see if he was okay.

"Is it safe?" the queen whispered, her trembling hand falling on Monica's wrist as if to prevent her from opening the door.

"I'm just going to peek," Monica assured her, the still silence from the other side providing no answers, making her sick with worry for Thad's welfare. She'd never forgive herself if he died before she got a chance to tell him how she truly felt about him.

How did she feel about him? She'd thought she was furious with him and assumed that meant she hated him more than anyone but Octavian himself. But the thought of him being shot made her realize she was angry with him because she cared about him. The depth of her anger was a clue to the depth of her feelings. If she hadn't cared about him to begin with, she wouldn't have felt so hurt when he left her. If she didn't have feelings for him still, then the thought of him being killed wouldn't have squeezed her heart so painfully.

Silently she turned the latch and let the door fall open just a crack.

Through the sliver of light she could see the king lying peacefully in his bed, apparently undisturbed as machines beeped and ticked in constant rhythm. The curtain blocked her view of anything beyond, save for a growing puddle of red that spread across the floor.

The curtain billowed. Someone was moving on the other side.

"Is it safe?" The queen's fingers gripped her arm.

"Monica?" Thad stepped past the curtain toward the bathroom.

"Thad!" She dived toward him. "Is it safe?"

"For now. I think." He stretched his arms out toward her.

"Are you all right? Were you shot?" She fought the urge to fling herself into his arms, unsure if she was welcome there, but desperate to hold him. The fear she felt for him rippled through her, and she reached for him.

"I'm fine." He pulled her close.

It wasn't until Monica got past the privacy curtain that she saw where the blood had originated.

A man in a jacket and slacks lay slumped on the floor. The nurses were gathered around him, but one had already shaken her head.

Monica tightened her hold on Thad, soaking up his solid strength, leaning on him as she fought to understand what had happened. "Is it Lucca?"

"It was. He tried to shoot the king." Thad held her tight.

She clung to him, grateful he was alive, more than aware that the body on the floor could have easily been his. A sob shuddered through her, and she whispered, "I'm so glad you're okay." She realized she still hadn't told him how she felt. But how did she feel? Exhausted and confused.

Thad smoothed her hair back from her face tenderly. "I'm so glad you're okay, too." He looked down at her with an expression far gentler than any she'd seen since he'd left her so long ago. But then he blinked and seemed to pull himself back into the situation.

Thad reached an arm toward his mother. "Lucca is dead," he said gently, blocking her from seeing the body on the floor. "He won't bother you again."

The queen shook her head, half trembling as she

leaned against her son for support. “Was anyone else hurt?”

“No.”

“Praise the Lord.” The queen’s voice gathered strength. “It’s too bad, though, that he won’t be able to answer any of our questions.”

“He answered a few of them before he went.” Thad nodded. “He said he’s controlled the king since the ambush, and he controls him still.”

“He controls the king,” Monica murmured, watching in disbelief as the nurses switched from trying to help Lucca, to checking the king’s vitals, which were unchanged.

One of the nurses addressed Thad. “Would you like us to have the general’s body removed?”

“The Sardis police will have to investigate to establish the cause of death.”

The woman nodded and stepped past them to leave, but Thad raised a hand, tipping his head thoughtfully at the woman. “Did you just refer to him as the general?”

“Yes. That’s General Lucca, isn’t it?”

“He’s not in uniform,” Monica murmured, even as Thad affirmed the woman’s identification.

“How did you know who he was?” Thad asked.

“He’s been pestering the doctor for days now.” Her words confirmed what Kirk had told them earlier.

“Wanting access to this room?”

The middle-aged nurse shrugged. "You'd have to ask the doctor about that." She wavered for a moment, as though torn between leaving and speaking.

Monica felt a prickle of suspicion. There was more to Lucca's involvement. He'd claimed the king had been under his control the whole time, hadn't he? "How do the doctor and the general know each other?"

"I'm not sure," the nurse admitted, a flicker of relief on her face, as though she'd wanted to say more, but hadn't been sure if her input was welcomed. Now she stepped closer to the three of them, and lowered her voice. "The general and the doctor, they were up to something. I can't say what for sure, but I'll tell you this—I've worked at this hospital long enough to know the drugs we usually administer in the case of a coma." She shook her head. "These levels are high. Higher than I've ever seen."

Petrela stepped gingerly through the doorway, and the nurse seemed to decide she was done talking, at least in their presence. "Would you like to talk to the doctor?"

Though Monica had initiated the line of questioning, Thad had taken to it quickly, and nodded. "I'd appreciate that." He turned to the general.

"I'll stay here," Petrela said, then nodded to him. "Let me know what you find out."

Monica squeezed Thad's hand. Was he really

going to leave Petrela alone in the room with his parents?

Thad must have recognized her concern, because he bent down and whispered in her ear, “Petrela shot Lucca. I take that to mean he’s on our side.” Kirk and Stasi approached from down the hall. “And Kirk can keep an eye on him. He’s armed.”

“I see.” Monica kept tight hold of Thad’s hand as he trailed the nurse out the door. Suspicions thumped with the pulse in her throat. She was too stunned by the sight of the dead body on the floor to know what to think. They met Kirk and Stasi midway down the hall, and Thad quickly explained their mission.

“It sounds as though this doctor may be keeping father in a medically induced coma. We’re going to look into it. Can you keep an eye on Petrela? He shot Lucca, but I’m still not completely convinced we can trust him.”

Stasi’s face bent with a wry smile. “Murder doesn’t exactly make him trustworthy—” she looked up at her brother with relief on her face “—but I am glad to hear that we don’t have to worry about Lucca anymore. When that shot went off, my heart stopped.”

The nurse hurried on ahead, and Monica gave Thad’s arm a tug. Much as she wanted to hear Kirk and Stasi’s take on this latest twist, she knew they needed to speak to the doctor. And she sensed he wasn’t going to hang around and wait to speak with them. Especially not if he'd been doing something they might disapprove of.

Thad broke away from the conversation and plowed past the guards beside her. A man in a doctor's coat stood by the nurses' station up ahead, clipboard in hand. He glanced up in their direction, then did a double take before dropping the clipboard. He reached across the nurses' station and appeared to curse under his breath before heading down the hall away from them at a brisk walk.

"Doctor!" The nurse attempted to wave him down. "We'd like to talk to you, Doctor!"

The man glanced back once more before breaking into a run.

As the nurse and Thad sped after him, Monica stopped at the nurses' station, which was unoccupied in the wake of the shooting down the hall. Already policemen in uniform were stepping off the elevator, adding to the confusion. As Thad had said, the Sardis police would need to investigate Lucca's death. But added to the many guards already filling the hallway, it made for a very crowded scene.

The clipboard sat where the doctor had dropped it, and Monica picked it up, flipping quickly through the pages, scanning them for names.

There was only one name on the pages, and it in no way resembled the king's name. But then, Monica realized, the doctor wouldn't have left behind incriminating evidence if he'd already had it in his hands. No, he'd looked across the nurses' station before making his retreat.

Monica looked in the direction that doctor had glanced, and saw several more clipboards protruding sideways from a small alcove under the countertop. Since no one else seemed to be paying her any attention, she quickly stepped through the nurses' station and flipped through the files on the clipboards.

Lydia, Philip.

Tucking the relevant clipboard under her arm, she headed back to find Kirk and Stasi to ask to borrow a phone. She had to get in touch with her father. The fact that both her parents had turned off their phones worried her. Had Octavian gone after them, as well? She prayed they were safe. More than that, she prayed there was some innocent explanation for their lifeless phones, and that she could talk to them after all. Her father might not be familiar with medical practice in Lydia, but he'd spent the past thirty years working as a doctor, mostly in the Intensive Care Unit.

He'd be able to tell if Philip's medication levels were off.

Thad raked his hand back through his hair as he made his way back to his father's hospital room. The doctor had evaded him—he'd swiped a card at a restricted doorway and slipped through before they could catch up to him. The nurse didn't have access to that area of the hospital, so Thad had to give up the chase.

Nor did the nurse seem to know enough about his father's medical situation to supply concrete direction.

"I don't know what it does," she admitted when he questioned her about his father's medication, "but we usually do two bags in the IV drip every twenty-four hours. Your father has been getting six bags. I thought it seemed funny, but what do I know? I'm just the nurse."

Thad thanked her for her help, then spotted his mother, still lingering in the hallway. She reached for him as he approached, and he pulled her into his arms.

"They're still investigating in there," she explained. After another moment's silence, she added, "Monica's trying to get in touch with her father, but she can't get ahold of him. She wants to run your father's medication schedule by him. She checked with another nurse, and the levels were all wrong. We can only assume it was due to Lucca's influence. But maybe, if we can get the medicine levels fixed..." Her voice drifted off.

"What are you saying?" Thad didn't want to let his hopes rise too high, but his mother's words sounded promising.

"If they can cut back the medication levels without shocking your father's system, and if the high levels haven't already done too much damage, and if his body is otherwise recovering from being shot—" faint hope filled her features "—there's a chance he might wake up."

While Thad absorbed the possible prognosis, one of the officers approached him and took his statement about the events that had led to Lucca's death. Much as Thad would have liked to stay out of the investigation—to stay out of the spotlight entirely—Lucca had robbed him of that option. Because he'd been closest to the generals the moment the gun had gone off, he was a witness to Lucca's death. He couldn't hide any longer.

The officers, at least, absorbed the revelation of his identity with discretion. He'd no more than finished talking with them, however, when Monica darted into the room, grabbing his arm. "Isabelle just called your sister. The paparazzi are headed to the hospital." She glanced back at Queen Elaine, who had taken up her post at the king's bedside. "Are there stairs this way?"

"Fire stairs. They lead to the parking garage." The queen gave them a conspiratorial look. "If the media arrive, I can hold them off," she promised, rising from her chair and following them into the hall.

Monica guided Thad around the corner, and they followed the fire exit signs.

"How did Isabelle know to warn us?"

"She's on her way to see your father right now.

She recognized some of the members of the media. It's impossible to say whether someone tipped them off that you're here, or if they're just following the scent of blood. But if they see you, that bit of stubble and the belief that you're dead might not fool them." They reached the bottom of the stairs, and Thad hesitated, wondering where they should go.

"This way." Monica waved a set of keys. "Kirk gave me his car keys. He said they'd catch a ride back with Isabelle, or someone." She depressed a button on the key fob, and parking lights flashed them a greeting.

"I can drive," Thad offered.

"Sorry." Monica cut him off from the driver's seat. "You've got to keep your head down."

While Monica backed the subcompact from the parking space, Thad obediently scooted into the backseat and sank down low, praying the nuisance reporters wouldn't slow them down too much. But at the same time, he almost smiled as he whispered to Monica, "We got away from Petrela."

She glanced back at him in the rearview mirror. "Are you going to try to go after the scepter?"

Thad didn't hesitate. "The sun will be setting shortly. This may be my only shot."

Though she'd earlier said she wanted to accompany him, Monica didn't ask if she could come along. She stayed silent, her eyes focused on guiding the car down the narrow ramp that led from the parking garage. "Should I head straight to the palace?" she asked once they reached the exit to the street.

"Not yet. If the paparazzi are swarming, they may be headed there, too. Let's wait until it gets dark out. Can you drive around a little?"

"Gladly."

Monica zipped up and down unfamiliar roadways. At least Kirk's car had plenty of gas in the tank. Finally, she was convinced she'd lost anyone who might be following them.

At the same time, she was also convinced *she* was lost.

"Um, Thad?" She brought the car to a stop at a scenic overlook high above the city. She'd instinctively gone uphill, hoping the vantage point would allow her to see her way back to the palace. "Do you know where we are?"

Thad had practically flattened himself against the upholstery to avoid being spotted, but he raised his head and made a face. "Lover's Lookout?"

A blush immediately rose to her cheeks. "Sorry. I got lost. It's starting to get dark out, and I thought perhaps if we could get high enough to see the city..."

"It's all right." Thad opened the back door and crawled out. "Let me stretch my legs and take a look around. I've only ever been here a time or two, and it was years ago, but I should be able to remember the way home."

Following his cue, Monica stepped out as well, stretching after the tense car ride before taking in the view.

They were high on a bluff overlooking the city, which twinkled below them as lights came on in windows and street corners, winking like yellow stars reflected in the waters of Sardis Bay. The Mediterranean stretched out like a rippling mirror, catching the reds and pinks and oranges of the setting sun, casting them back like a thank offering hurled to the heavens.

A canopy of tree branches above them and fragrant climbing flowers framed the image, and Monica couldn't help drawing in a deep breath. "It's so lovely," she murmured softly, sitting down on the hood of the car.

Thad took a few steps closer to her, but his attention remained on the vista before them. "My domain." Irony stung his words. "The kingdom I defend."

Finally, Monica thought, *a moment to speak to Thad, alone.* She swallowed past the lump that had risen to her throat, and tried to find the words.

"If we head east down this road—" Thad had already moved on to finding a way home "—I believe we'll come to a cross street that leads downtown. From there, it's no trouble to get back to the palace."

He stepped closer to her and reached out his hand. “Would you like me to drive? It’s getting dark, so hopefully no one will see me.”

Monica stared at his outstretched hand for a moment. No wedding ring. No sign that he’d ever worn one. She, too, had removed hers before returning home to her parents. No sense giving anyone a reason to ask questions she didn’t have the heart to answer.

Thad cleared his throat. “We should get going. Every minute is precious.”

“You’re right.” She handed over the keys, surprised how reluctant she felt to leave Lover’s Lookout and such a gorgeous sunset. She knew the clock was ticking and her son’s life was on the line. So why did she long to lean against Thad’s shoulder and linger in the light of the sinking sun?

Thad took the keys from her hands, but didn’t move.

She looked up at him, thinking that perhaps he’d taken a moment to bask in the glow of the beauty around them. Instead she found him looking down at her as though she was the dazzling beauty.

“Thad?”

He shook his head slowly, shushing her, and traced the outline of her face with the tips of his fingers. He stopped at her chin and tilted her head upward a tiny nudge.

Without really thinking about it, she rose up on

her tiptoes and brought their faces closer together. His lips brushed hers with a sweetness that whispered of promises neither of them could keep. He let out a plaintive, almost inaudible moan. Then he took two steps backward before circling around the car to the driver's side door.

Monica wanted to reach for him, to pull him close again. At the very least, she wanted to confess her jumbled feelings. She longed to hear what Thad was thinking and feeling, to learn if the man she'd once loved so deeply was still buried inside his banished and battered frame.

She pushed the longing aside. This was no time to let her emotions get the best of her. Until they had the scepter in their hands, there wasn't any time to waste. Besides, if she wanted to talk to Thad about her jumbled feelings, they could always talk in the car.

But once Thad had the vehicle headed down the road, Monica still couldn't find the words. *Please, God,* she prayed silently, *help me know what to say.*

Finally she turned in her seat enough to see Thad's profile as he focused on the road, and she cleared her throat. "I'm sorry."

"It's no big deal. We'll be back at the palace shortly."

"Not for getting lost." She sucked in a shaking breath and plowed on, in spite of her trembling heart. "For getting mad at you. For accusing you of running away." She'd heard Lucca's words from the tiny hospital bathroom, and realized that she'd spoken the same accusation that Thad's murderous enemy had used against him. "You did what you thought was best. I realize that now."

"No. I was wrong to run away. I should have faced Octavian years ago."

"Could you have defeated him then?"

"Can I defeat him now?" Thad's mouth twitched as he stared straight ahead, shifting with the manual transmission as they crawled through the first of a series of stoplights.

"Can you?" Monica whispered into the fear-filled silence.

"I don't see how."

His prognosis fell like the blade of a guillotine, cutting off her hope. Frantically, she scrambled to think of a reason why they ought to be able to defeat Octavian. Surely Lucca's death counted for something. "Do you think General Petrela is on our side?"

"If he is, even Octavian will know it after what happened at the hospital today."

"Who's going to tell Octavian?"

"Any one of the men in the hallway could."

"They didn't intervene when Petrela shot Lucca."

"I could have been shot. My father could have been shot." Thad punched the car into gear. "And they did nothing. They're nothing but mercenaries. Octavian has hundreds of them—enough to defeat the Lydian Army, if it came to a battle. We are outnumbered, outmaneuvered and he has our son."

Monica felt her hope receding like an ocean drawn back by the tide, sucked away by an invisible force, each wave a futile effort to escape the immutable pull from beyond. "God won't let my son be taken from me."

"He already has."

Tears rolled down her cheeks, but Monica could think of nothing else to say. Up ahead, she could see the dark shadows of the palace walls looming through the darkness. Her heart hurt for Thad. In the bitterness of his words, she could taste the despair he'd been living in. She wished she could take that pain away from him and give him back his faith, but she didn't know how. "What happened, Thad? What made you so angry at God?"

Thad remained silent. Realizing her words—a desperate plea for him to open up to her—might have sounded somewhat accusational, she softened her tone. "I want to understand," she whispered as they neared the palace.

After a painful stretch of silence, Thad eased the car through the back palace gates and brought it to a stop in an open, empty bay of the garage. "I don't want you to understand."

His response was so unexpected, she sputtered. "Why not?"

The silence was deeper with the engine dead, and

the sounds of the city blocked out by the high wall that encircled the palace grounds. The darkness had deepened as night had fallen, and inside the garage was pitch-black, the stinging scent of burnt gasoline far too reminiscent of the oil rig where she'd found him. Monica couldn't see Thad's face.

"Because—" his voice echoed from somewhere in the utter darkness "—if you *understand,*" he said, straining against the words until she could almost hear his angry grip on the steering wheel, "that's what Octavian wants. He wants you to spark that hope inside me so I'll chase after it. He wants me to abandon reason in favor of love. He wants me to care more about you than my kingdom, and *I can't allow myself to do that.* I shouldn't have kissed you back there. I was too weak to resist. I'm too weak to defeat Octavian, too."

Monica sat in shocked silence, the garage vapors and vast darkness reminiscent of what Thad must have lived through for six long years at the edge of the earth, reminding himself daily of all he'd given up, and all he would never get back. Something warm and tragic stirred in her lungs, and she felt like that fish on the rocky Alaskan shoreline, flopping helplessly, wanting to live, but beyond all hope.

While she sat still, absorbing what he'd said, Thad got out and headed toward the palace. Monica sighed and trudged after him. They'd used up nearly all of the time Octavian had given them, and she felt as though they were further away from succeeding now than they'd been in the beginning.

Worse yet, she supposed that was precisely what Octavian wanted them to feel.

NINE

Thad dressed in black to blend in with the darkness. He slipped his phone into his pocket and tried to think of anything else he might need.

Comfortable shoes for walking, even jogging. It was a long journey, making it a long night. He brought a flashlight, even an extra flashlight, just in case something happened to the first one, and slipped a bottle of water into one cargo pocket of his pants. Then, feeling lopsided, he slid another bottle into the pocket on the other leg.

There really wasn't anything else.

With time ticking relentlessly away, Thad headed through the palace to the entrance of the tunnel that would take him to the place he'd left the scepter six years before. And if he found it, for once he'd have bested Octavian. It might not mean he'd get his son back, but it would at least give him a shot.

And if the scepter was gone, he'd have to come up with another plan, though he couldn't imagine what that might be.

The soft soles of his black cross-training sneakers made no sound as he slipped down the empty palace halls, past tapestries, framed artwork, pillars with vases and the occasional suit of armor worn by the kings of old. When he came to the open throne room, he paused, his back against the wall, panting.

Had he heard footsteps?

Perhaps it was just the urgent beat of his heart, driving him to hurry, or maybe the echo of his own footsteps against the cold stone floors.

He glanced into the wide throne room, where at the age of twenty-two he'd signed the Article of the Crown, confirming his intention to rule Lydia should anything happen to his father, who'd then just been crowned king. And then the paper was rolled up and tucked back inside the Scepter of Charlemagne, and stored away in a locked case until he'd taken it two years later, hiding it away from Octavian.

This same throne room was where Octavian wanted to meet with him in less than fourteen hours. In this same throne room, he'd face the man who'd stolen his son.

Somehow, he had to protect them both—his son, and the crown. But what if he couldn't do both? What if he had to choose?

Light from the rising moon spilled in through the stained-glass windows high on the walls of the vaulted throne room, pouring in and landing on the glass case that held the crown of Lydia. The amethysts sparkled lifelessly, their cold light unchanged from that day when he'd signified his intent to rule Lydia with faith, honor and love.

Love.

He'd been naive to think it could ever be that simple.

Shaking his head, he darted across the throne room, tripping down the shallow stairs that led to a back hallway. If he turned left, he'd end up back at the front of the palace. Turning right instead, he ducked into a chamber that was mostly used for storage, the wooden wall panels camouflaging the secret door in the corner. Further obscured by a stack of tables that nearly blocked the way, the door itself had no knob, but was opened by sliding the framework of the jamb out of the way, each piece in ordered succession, like a massive brain-teaser puzzle.

Thad pulled one of the flashlights from a cargo pocket, and held the light steady between his teeth while he slid the panels to the side. As soon as the door settled back in place behind him, gravity would close the jamb back around it, as though the way had never been opened to the tiny room beyond.

There was nothing there to give anyone who made it that far any indication that there might be more to the space than stale, forgotten air. Certainly nothing to hint that the side wall could be pushed back just far enough to reveal a small handle on the floor, which, when pulled, raised a trapdoor. And no one would ever guess that from that trapdoor, stone steps led down in darkness to an ancient tunnel under the sea.

Monica held the wooden jamb just far enough to the side so that, blinking with one eye at the crack, she could see Thad shuffling in the beam of his flashlight in a tiny room on the other side. Knowing he didn't want her coming with him, but determined to see their mission through to the end, she'd decided to follow him.

He never had to know she was behind him. As long as he didn't need her help, she wouldn't let on that she was there. But the burning in her heart told her she *had* to come. For one thing, there was no way she could possibly sleep knowing what Thad was up to. And besides that, Octavian had given her the mission to retrieve the scepter, just as much as he'd given it to Thad.

Peter's life depended on the scepter. So she had no choice but to follow Thad, even though there was every chance he'd be furious with her if he found out she'd gone against his wishes.

His wishes didn't matter. All that mattered was the scepter, and getting Peter back, safe and sound. So she watched Thad, taking great care not to make the slightest sound that would give away her presence.

What was he doing, shoving at the wall? What

was that he tugged at on the floor? Monica wondered if she'd be able to open the secret doors he'd passed through, but there was no way she could find out until he was gone. If he realized she was following him, he'd only send her back. They'd only end up wasting time.

And they didn't have time to waste.

Thad settled the trapdoor back into place above his head. He then pushed hard on the levered hinge that would move the wall above back over the handle of the trapdoor, effectively disguising his escape route. There would be nothing to give away where he'd gone. It would be as though he had passed straight through the thick stone walls and disappeared.

He turned his attention to the steps, which bent in a narrow trail downward, their steep descent almost ladderlike in places, as the tunnel descended to a level far beneath the sea.

Of course, when this tunnel had been first carved hundreds of years before, the sea hadn't been there. The king's castle that sat now in ruins on the Island of Dorsi had originally been built at the tip of a peninsula. But violent storms and ravaging waves had long before washed away the sandy shores, carving out waterways along the slender strip of land, leaving an archipelago of islands stretching out beyond the city of Sardis.

The storms and waves hadn't touched the tunnel, chiseled, as it was, through stolid stone beneath the bottom of the sea.

All the upheaval had, however, shifted the tunnel's path in places, so that the corridor, once an even meter wide by nearly two meters high, jutted in on itself, nearly blocking its own way at times, so that Thad had to turn sideways to squeeze through or duck to crawl under low-dipping ledges, shuffling nearly on his knees.

He was scooting along this way, crawling several body lengths ahead with his flashlight in his teeth, reminding himself that he'd gotten over his claustrophobia years before, when he heard a hollow boom behind him, and froze.

It could be the sea. He'd spotted trickling water between the blocks here and there, and stepped through puddles and over trails of lime and distilled salt where water had slowly oozed, filling in its own path with sediment behind it.

There was nothing to say the archaic channel wouldn't be breached by the sea at any moment, filled with water like an aqueduct, drowning anyone unfortunate enough to be caught inside.

Certainly it was possible—Thad found it remarkable that it hadn't already happened years before. The only reason the tunnel had survived this long was that no one knew about it, and no one used it.

Had he disturbed it enough with his shuffling along that the stones above him were starting to crack?

If he had, it was likely too late to escape going backward. And there wasn't nearly enough time to make it out the other end, not if water started gushing in behind him.

No, all there was left was to soldier steadily onward, regardless of how hopeless the situation was. It wasn't as though any of it mattered anyway. Even if he found the scepter, even if he brought it safely back, there was no reason to believe he could use it to get his son back.

There were really only two choices left to him: to give up completely or to keep crawling, no matter how endless the tunnel seemed.

He stopped, and the cold stone bit into his knees uncomfortably. The chill of the subterranean rocks crept its way up his arms with a dull ache.

No, giving up was no good. It was too painful.

He pictured Monica standing on the oil platform, her tired eyes telling him she'd thought about retreating, her worn-out words repeating the mantra she'd no doubt recited countless times.

I've traveled too far to turn around now.

He tried out the words in a whisper. They fit just fine, exhaling with every sigh and grunt of effort, tripping off his tongue at a faster pace as the ceiling arched upward again, high enough for him to walk upright, and then to charge forward at something approximating a run.

I've traveled too far to turn around now.

Monica had frozen when the trapdoor settled back into place with a loud boom.

Thad had to have heard it, even if he was far ahead of her by now.

His light had disappeared in the distance and, reluctant as she was to give her position away, she figured if she couldn't see the beam of his torch, he wouldn't be able to see hers, either.

She clicked on her tiny flashlight and started moving as quickly as she dared. She didn't want to catch up to Thaddeus, but neither did she want to give away her presence. Every so often she paused, listening, turning off her light and squinting ahead, trying to determine how close she'd come to her husband.

A trickling drip of water met her ears, an unsettling reminder that the tunnel they journeyed through was very old, and apparently less than stable. Had she been foolish to follow Thaddeus? What if something happened to her?

She thought about turning around. The warm bed in her palace suite had soft sheets and more than enough comfortable pillows.

But where was Peter sleeping tonight?

And how would she ever get him back if she didn't keep going?

Words echoed back to her through the tunnel, so familiar she almost thought they'd come from inside her, instead of without.

"I've traveled too far to turn around now."

She recognized that voice, and felt a tightening in her chest. Thad was up there, trudging onward, for Peter's sake. She wasn't sure precisely why she felt such a strong need to accompany him, but she wasn't about to let him make the journey alone.

Whenever the tunnel passage allowed it, Thad kept to a steady jog. The narrow trail crept for miles under the archipelago, hand-chiseled through solid rock by hundreds of workers over the course of several decades. Though a marvelous feat of architecture, it wasn't as long as some modern undersea tunnels, such as the one that connected London and Paris, or another he'd heard of in Japan. Unlike those, however, which were dozens of meters in diameter, wide enough to fit trains and large machinery, the tunnel that ran to the Island of Dorsi had been carved just wide enough to permit two average-sized adults to walk side by side.

In that respect, it reminded him more of Hezekiah's Tunnel, the famous aqueduct-turned-escape-hatch that had been chiseled under Jerusalem around 700 BC, and still drew hordes of tourists every year.

Knowing Hezekiah's tunnel was both older and more heavily traveled made Thad feel slightly less foolhardy for attempting the underground trip alone.

Unlike Hezekiah's tunnel, however, the long passage to Dorsi had shifted over the years, and in places threatened to give way again. It had only three entrances: the opening in the palace, through which he'd entered, the distant exit on Dorsi, and a short spur on the Lydia mainland, which opened to a narrow cave on the sheer cliffs north of the Sardis marina. He passed the spur without hesitation. There was nothing for him to gain by going that way.

As Thad plodded onward, he came to a section where the smooth floor of the tunnel was littered with smaller crumbling rocks.

A smattering of pebbles rained down as his footfalls echoed against the floor.

He slowed his pace. Above him, cracks crisscrossed the stones like fissures in a sheet of ice. He placed his fingers in one of the gaps. His whole hand slid in easily, but let out a yelp of surprise as the stones squeezed inward, applying gentle pressure on his fingers before releasing them like an exhaled sigh.

Thad pulled his hand out quickly. The tunnel seemed to be shifting, almost like a living, breathing thing. It wasn't rigid at all, but flexible, moaning and sighing with the pulse of the tide and the ocean waves far above. That, Thad realized, was likely the secret to its long survival. It wasn't brittle. It gave under pressure, like an earthquake-proof building, engineered to sway instead of snap.

Another crack inched its way upward toward the ceiling, and Thad felt the length of it, relieved to find no trace of moisture that would have indicated close proximity to the sea above. At least here the salt water wasn't threatening to rush in. Most likely the tunnel ran under one of the islands at this point, instead of the sea.

Deciding to test his theory on the flexibility of the tunnel walls, Thad wedged his fingers in the vertical chasm. Again, he felt the stone move inward, squeezing his fingers. This time, however, the pinch felt tighter, and he quickly tugged his fingers free before they could be smashed. To his relief, the stones shifted under the pressure from his hands, rather than crushing him. One of the large sections of stone moved to the side as he drew his hand back.

Then a few more pebbles rained down.

Thad stumbled backward as the stone he'd inadvertently dislodged shifted inward, the loosened rocks behind it giving way under hundreds of years of pressure. Thad watched in disbelief as the crumbling wall rained down.

At the last moment, he jumped away from the avalanche he'd triggered. But he wasn't quite quick enough. Falling stones, ranging in size from marble to baseball, and some even larger, poured from the widening gap, quickly filling the narrow tunnel, burying him up to his chest.

Dust filled his nostrils and coated his lips. He pinched his eyes shut. When he opened them, he realized his flashlight had been buried, as well. In the darkness every sound was amplified. The pattering of the last loosened stones gradually gave way to silence.

Thad blinked, straining his eyes to see, but there was no light to aid his sight. His right arm, which held the flashlight, was completely buried. He'd pulled his left hand up toward the ceiling at the last minute, and now his hand rested above the pile of rocks.

He was buried, the crush of stones so tight he struggled to breathe. Searching by feel with his one free hand, Thad explored the mound that all but covered him. The stones toward the top were large and heavy, and he shoved at the nearest one, feeling feeble as the angle of his arm permitted him to apply only the strength of his triceps and forearm muscles.

Pushing at the rock, he managed to get it to budge just an inch before he gave up, panting. What had he done? Why had he stopped to inspect the side of the tunnel? Granted, he was an engineer, and the marvel of ancient handiwork had intrigued him, but he was supposed to be on a mission.

He was supposed to claim the scepter.

And now he was underground, buried under a pile

of rocks from which he might never be able to work himself free, the cold of the stones already seeping past his skin, cramping his immobile limbs. He was stuck—buried, quite possibly forever. And even if he did manage to get free after days and days, Octavian would be long gone with Peter by then.

What if he couldn't work himself free? The tunnel was a secret known only to himself and his father. His father was in a coma and might never wake up—and if he did, he might not remember anything, certainly not such a trivial detail like the tunnel.

Perhaps his family members would simply think he'd sneaked away again, off to some other corner of the earth, while all the time there he was beneath them, fighting for his breath in a tunnel that seemed more and more like a tomb.

Monica, of course, would assume he'd failed her again.

The thought pinched his heart even harder than the prognosis of being buried alive, left to die a slow death from cold and thirst. Monica would never know that he hadn't meant to fail her, that he'd had every intention of *trying* to get her son back, even if the odds had been against him from the start.

Monica would think he was a coward who had run away. She would never know how much she'd meant to him or how the memories of the love they'd shared had warmed him in the frozen north, keeping him safe through dark nights that lasted for months.

He felt a tear trail its way down the dust on his cheek as he recalled the sight of her, sitting tense on the plane, hoping against hope that she'd get Peter back. What had she said then?

The earth is the Lord's and everything in it.

Like the fissure in the stone, the words cracked through the hardened walls inside him. Did everything on earth, even under the earth, really belong to God? Could God really move mountains, even mountains made of fallen rocks?

Thad rebelled against the thought. He'd put his trust in God before, praying daily that God would release him from the prison of the frozen north, that God would set him free from exile and return him to his family and everyone he loved.

But God hadn't budged.

The earth is the Lord's and everything in it.

If that were true, God should have seen him, even on the oil rig north of Alaska, and answered his prayers. But God had remained silent.

A cry for help rose inside him, but Thad pinched it back. What good would it do to pray now? No one could hear him. Nothing could come of it.

The pressure on his heart grew harder, but he told himself it was just from the stones. There was nothing to be gained by trusting God. There was absolutely nothing that could come from crying out for help. No one would hear him. To believe otherwise was as absurd as thinking that He really cared.

God didn't care, and there was no one to help him. So Thad kept his lips sealed shut.

Monica paused at the intersection, debating which way to go. No matter how closely she listened, she couldn't hear Thad moving up ahead, nor could she detect any sign of his footprints on the solid stone floor. Perhaps she should turn around while she still knew the way? She'd seen at least one spur branching off from the main line. How many more paths bisected hers ahead? If she got lost in the tunnels she might never find her way out.

Suddenly she heard a rumble like falling stones ahead, and instinctively she scrambled backward. The narrow tunnel was spooky enough. Hollow rattling and falling stones made it a thousand times worse.

Pointing her flashlight back the way she came, she pondered turning around.

After all, if the tunnel gave way and she was never heard from again, who would be there for Peter, assuming they ever got him back? The simple fact was, she didn't like the tunnel, and any excuse to get out was good enough for her.

And yet, Thad was up there somewhere, alone. He'd probably caused the rockfall she'd heard. What if it had closed off the path between her and him? Then there would be no point in moving forward again.

She might as well turn and go back.

Torn between moving onward and turning around, Monica stood still and prayed silently for God to guide her steps.

How long she stood like that, exhausted from a full day, she wasn't sure. It felt like a long time, and her prayer for guidance blended into prayers for Peter's safety, and prayers for Thad, that God would keep him safe.

Then she pointed the beam of her flashlight back the way she'd come, and started retracing her steps as she made her way toward the hidden room in the palace, and ultimately, to the soft bed that waited for her.

A creaking noise behind her stopped her moments later, and she wondered if the tunnel wasn't about to cave in again, this time possibly worse. About to make a run for it, she heard the creaking noise again.

But it wasn't so much a creaking noise as it was a creaky voice, dry and raspy and worn.

She had to listen carefully to understand what it said.

Help.

With a start, she realized it was Thad's voice.

She pointed her flashlight back down the main branch of the tunnel, and ran toward her husband's cries for help.

Thad felt foolish crying out, pinned as he was in darkness, with only partial use of one arm. He felt almost foolish enough to laugh at himself, but then he realized the laughter rising inside him didn't come from embarrassment at all.

Light filtered in through the cracks in his heart, easing the burden he'd been carrying. It made no sense that he should laugh, not with everything so bleak and the tunnel in utter darkness, but the relief he felt inside his heart was palpable. Somehow, in crying out for help, he'd admitted that he couldn't do it all himself.

That he needed God's help.

That he believed God could help him.

Somehow, in crying out for help, he'd eased the burden that had weighed him down since he'd run off to save Lydia all by himself.

Perhaps he didn't have to save Lydia all by himself.

Perhaps he didn't have to be alone anymore.

And perhaps it didn't matter, because the realization had come too late. He was alone, buried by his own stubborn stupidity in a tomb carved from darkness.

"Help!" He raised the cry again, and this time he heard something more than his own solitary voice echoing back.

"I'm coming. Stay right there."

The laughter spilled out of him, running with his tears in dusty trails down his face until he realized he was sobbing like a child. He saw a light bobbing toward him through his streaming tears, and he called out, "I'm not going anywhere."

Monica picked her way up the mound of rocks toward him, pointing her flashlight beam upward so that it reflected back indirect light, illuminating the pile. She nestled it into place between a couple of larger stones, then set to work scooping rocks out of the way, letting them slide down the pile behind her.

"Careful—don't dislodge any more of the tunnel wall," he cautioned.

"I don't think there's room for anything more to go anywhere, even if it wanted to be dislodged," she panted, hauling some of the larger stones down the slope of the pile.

She didn't ask him how he'd gotten in his predicament, or chide him for being foolish enough to venture through the tunnel alone. He watched her work in silence, marveling that she'd come to him from out of nowhere, even though he'd insisted on making the journey alone.

When she got the rocks clear from his left arm so he could use it to help, he started pushing rocks out of the way with her.

Together, they sent a large block skidding down the pile.

While Monica caught her breath, Thad settled into the reality of the hope her presence provided.

"Thank you," he told her.

"It's no problem." She was already at work pushing another boulder. "I'll need a hand with this one, too."

As he applied as much push as he could leverage against the stubborn rock, he clarified, "Thank you for not listening when I said you couldn't come with me. Thank you for following me." The rock came loose from its stubborn hold and slid down the slope, pushing several smaller stones ahead of it.

Thad tried to help Monica as much as he could, but there was little he could do in his position, and his whole body felt bruised and achy cold, so instead he watched her work steadily to free him, and felt gratitude swelling in his injured heart.

As her face moved close to his, he imagined reaching for her, pulling her into his embrace, kissing her as he had kissed her so long ago.

Instead he did what he could to shove the rocks away, feeble though his efforts seemed. But with Monica's help, the hill of rocks slid gradually lower.

And then he could move his torso and twist, and soon the slender beams from his buried flashlight pierced their way up through the swirling dust, widening like the rivers that had once split the peninsula into islands, until the light filled the tunnel as the sea had covered the sand.

Once she had his other arm free, he was able to move rocks with both hands, forcing the blood to flow again through his numb limbs, feeling sensation return in stinging spears down his wrists, through his hands, to the tips of his fingers. Finally he was able to reach the water bottle tucked into the pocket of his right leg. The plastic had been dented but wasn't broken, and the cool water washed the thick dust from his throat.

He handed Monica the bottle and she drank quickly before getting right back to work.

Finally he could lift his knees, and stomped his way upward until the stones had shifted and slipped into the places where his feet had been, and he stood on top of them, feeling light-headed as the blood once again flowed freely to his toes.

"Let's get moving." He pointed his flashlight beam toward Dorsi, and prayed that by walking, he'd recover full feeling in his feet and legs.

"Are you sure you want to go on?" Monica looked hesitant.

"I've got to recover the scepter."

"But what if there's another cave-in? What if it's water next time?"

She'd no doubt spotted the trickling wetness at other points along the tunnel, and guessed they ran beneath the sea.

"I brought this one upon myself," he admitted. "But with you here to keep me from poking my hands where they shouldn't be, we should be fine."

She smiled at him. Even with her eyes rimmed with dust, she was beautiful.

"Shall we go, then?" Thad was eager to get moving before he acted on the urge to kiss her. Ever since he'd relented to calling out for help, ever since hope had sprung inside him at the realization that Monica was there and he wasn't going to die, everything inside him had gone all mushy. Part of him wanted to pray and sing and kiss her and dance around like a fool.

And if he didn't get moving, he just might give in to those impulses.

Fortunately, Monica headed forward with him, and they trotted along beside each other, moving as quickly as they dared without dislodging any more stones. To his relief, it seemed the farther they went, the more solid the tunnel became. The worst damage appeared to be near the start where the shoreline had broken away from the islands.

Finally, they reached a set of stone steps that twisted upward at a steep climb, and Thad was forced to stoop down low in places as the ceiling curved around above them. The spiral narrowed until it came to rest at a stone ledge, and a wall blocked the way completely.

"Now what?" Monica pointed her flashlight at each corner, which settled flush against the surrounding stones as though the way ended completely.

Thad caught his breath and tried to remember. He'd only come this way once, and it had been starting from the other side.

"This stone panel slides to the left from the other side. So from this side, it should go right." He tucked his fingers along the chiseled edge of the stone, and pulled.

"Isn't that heavy?" Monica looked impressed at how easily he slid the stone to the side.

"It's a false stone, chiseled thin like a veneer." He scooted out through the narrow gap, just wide enough to allow his broad shoulders to pass.

Monica started to follow him.

"Wait." He squinted in the bright moonlight. "Let me make absolutely certain we're alone. Secrecy is imperative at this point."

"I understand." Monica ducked her head back.

Thad circled around the castle ruins, grateful for the bright moonlight that illuminated the island. There were no boats in the inlet, no sign that anyone had been there since his friend Kirk had taken Stasi to Dorsi, using the island as a refuge after the ambush.

It was a good place to hide. He'd spent a few weeks there, himself, hiding from his father and Octavian, trying to decide how to get away before he'd settled on being an engineer on the oil rigs. How many times had he sat on these very rocks, feeling the same warm ocean breeze kiss his cheeks, wishing Monica could be there with him? He'd been so tempted to bring her to stay with him, but what would that have accomplished? Shortly thereafter, he'd gone to Alaska, and she couldn't have come with him there. He'd done the best he could, given the circumstances.

As he looked across the crumbling stones, Thad thought of the stories he could tell Monica, the hidden corners of the ancient castle, the vistas he'd like to share. There was so much about the island he wanted to show her and tell her. But now was not the time. He needed to hurry.

Thad pulled out his phone to check the time. It was nearly four in the morning. They'd taken forever traveling through the tunnel, and unburying him from the rocks. He stared at the glowing numbers and wished he could turn them back, but they moved relentlessly forward, bringing him ever closer to the showdown with Octavian.

The virtual clock hand made its circuit across the face of his phone, while a little symbol in the corner detected the nearest satellite, assuring him that, as promised, he had coverage if he wanted to place a call. Thad looked up at the starry sky, and saw a satellite above, its light larger, its body closer than the stars, winking at him, almost as though it recognized his phone's signal and sent its greetings from the sky.

Shoving the phone back in his pocket, Thad got to work. He had to find the scepter and return to the palace, and hatch a plan to save his son.

"Can I come out?" Monica whispered from the tunnel entrance.

Thad hesitated. It would be lovely for her to stand next to him on the Island of Dorsi, to drink in the sights and smells of the moonlit paradise. But then, just as he'd been tempted to investigate the cracks in the tunnel walls, he'd be tempted to show her around the island. More than that, he'd give in to the ever-growing temptation to pull her into his arms and make up for the six years they'd lost.

But surely she wouldn't welcome his touch, not as long as their son was still in Octavian's clutches. She hated him for causing Peter's kidnapping.

He'd only be wasting his time trying to woo her.

They didn't have time to waste.

"No. I'll be right there. One minute."

Of course, it ended up taking more than a minute. By the time he found the corner and the stone he'd marked with a cross, and then counted over and up according to the numbers in his wedding anniversary date, and located the stone he'd wedged back into place six years before, it had to have been twenty minutes, maybe more. He looked over to see Monica dozing in the tiny doorway, and he was glad she'd taken the opportunity to rest.

He still had his work cut out for him.

There was the trouble of digging the stone from the mortar, and finding the tools he'd hidden elsewhere in the queen's tower, working the stone free and pulling it back to reveal the compartment in the wall, and the slender stick hiding there, as still and innocent as the coordinating crown he'd passed in the throne room earlier.

He grabbed it up, holding it out in the moonlight just long enough to feel the rush of triumph pulsing through his veins, unfamiliar hope surging through him in a heady burst.

And then the silence throbbed with a relentless pulse, and Thad felt dread and panic fill him instead. He looked around frantically as the air around him began to thrum, agitating the balmy air, whipping it to violent thrashing.

A helicopter buzzed toward the island, shattering the darkness with its bright search lights, flashing across the stone walls like searching hands until they locked on him and he looked up, caught in their brilliant glare.

He'd been spotted.

TEN

Monica woke with a start. She gasped as the sound that had tugged her from sleep grew louder and lights swirled overhead before locking their beams on Thaddeus. She saw his knuckles whiten as he clenched the scepter and watched him glance from a dislodged hole in the wall to her hiding place among the rocks, and back up to the sky.

She could feel the battle that waged inside him, knowing that if Octavian took away the scepter, they'd lose everything.

And just as quickly, she felt Thad ticking off his options. He couldn't hide the scepter in the hole inside the wall, because they'd see him do it and know where he'd put it. He couldn't pass it off to Monica, because he'd give away the tunnel under the palace, thereby exposing her and everyone at the other end to Octavian's endless reach. The tunnel was a trap, and Thad turned his back to her, resolutely signaling that he understood that he had to keep her hiding place a secret at all costs.

He couldn't toss it into the sea, because they'd only watch where it landed and dive in after it. It was too big to hide in his pockets. In fact, he didn't dare let it go.

She watched as he did the only thing he possibly could do. He held the scepter tight in his hands and stood his ground, ready to take on whoever came at him.

Fear stole her breath as she watched the helicopter hover above the island, men pouring down the ladder toward Thaddeus. With gratitude, she realized they must be under orders not to shoot him or at least not to kill him on purpose. After all, they still needed his signature or would prefer it. But if it came down to losing the scepter or killing Thad, she could guess which Octavian would pick.

No doubt the men had been made aware of his preference, too.

Prayers poured from her lips as Thad kicked high in the air, knocking the first man from the ladder before his feet ever hit the ground. The man landed with a sickening crunch and didn't get up.

The next dark figure leaped from above, lunging at Thad as he fell through the air toward him.

Thad stepped to the side and let him fall, turning to face him as he landed. Thad swung a punch before the man was steady on his feet, and had the advantage for all of his three-punch fight. The man went down and Thad looked up.

There were three more men on the ladder, and the bottom one hesitated, as though trying to decide how best to descend, or whether he wanted to descend at all. Monica prayed more fervently, grateful that the men could only descend one at a time, that the helicopter couldn't land among the jagged stones of the castle ruins.

The third man came at Thad kicking, but once again Thad managed to stay back from the thrashing boots until his assailant had twisted himself around and nearly landed. Then a high back kick caught the attacker in the shoulder, hammering him into a nearby stone wall. But the man wasn't out, and the next figure was already leaping toward Thad.

Monica pinched her dry eyes shut against the dust-swirled air stirred up by the thrashing rotor blades. When she opened her eyes a second later, Thad staggered with a man clinging to his back, gloved hands tight around his neck, and he ran backward against a wall, ramming his attacker against the stones just as the last man dropped from the ladder.

Thad braced himself against the wall, crushing the man behind him as he kicked out with both feet, catching his latest assailant full in the chest, sending him reeling backward. Then Thad lunged backward again, and the man who'd been clinging to his back sagged to the ground.

Just in time, Thad rushed at the last man, throwing a punch toward his jaw. The figure recoiled, and Thad finished him with another punch.

But already two of the men on the ground staggered to their feet, and Monica watched in horror as Thad struggled to catch his breath, to stand up straight, while the men rushed at him.

Thad leaped to the side as they pounced, then threw a quick kick behind him, sending the first man into the second. They swayed only slightly before rushing him as a team.

Surely intent on keeping the scepter as far from them as possible, Thad turned his back toward them and unleashed a pattern of kicks that kept them at bay. But at the same time, the men he'd already pushed aside rushed at him again. Even as Thad pushed the other two back, his persistent attackers piled upon him.

Monica looked around frantically, trying to spot a weapon, or anything she could use against Thad's attackers. There were loose rocks everywhere, and she scooted out of the hole, staying to the shadows, shuffling off to the right, where a parapet had once promised the castle guards cover while defending the royal family.

They would provide her the same cover tonight. Quickly she plucked up two baseball-sized rocks and hurled them with unleashed fury at the men who groped for the scepter.

The first hit a man in the back, and though it appeared to startle him, he hardly twitched.

Monica realized they were likely wearing body armor.

Fine, then. Their heads were exposed. Peter had been intent on learning how to throw a baseball all summer. She'd gotten pretty good at pitching it accurately into his mitt. Granted, she was throwing with a lot more force now, but she also had a lot more at stake, and plenty of pent-up fury to propel the rocks with pummeling force.

She pulled back and let loose a chunk of rock.

It hit a man on the back of the head just as he reached for the scepter. For a second his hands hovered, outstretched in the air, giving her the opportunity to send a second missile knocking against his ear. He fell.

But even as Monica felt a surge of triumph at her success, she glanced toward Thaddeus in time to see him crumple under a mighty blow.

There were only two men still standing, plus those on the ground who still moaned and writhed as though they might yet suck up the strength to pull themselves to their feet again. Monica could only guess at the compelling prize Octavian had offered for the man who returned with the scepter.

The men fighting Thaddeus had pushed him backward, and they were now too far away for her to hit them with any accuracy from behind the protective cover of the parapets. She hated to risk showing herself, but there was nothing else for it. Already one man had hold of the scepter, prying it out of Thad's hands, while the other pummeled her husband's midsection with flying fists.

An arsenal of rocks cradled in her left arm, Monica scuttled out from behind the wall and hurled a stone at the man who'd grabbed the scepter. He looked stunned, but didn't fall.

Her missiles were losing force as her arms grew tired, but all she had to do was remember what she was fighting for, and she found the strength to hurl the next rock harder. Pitching it at the man who punched her husband, she caught him in the back of the head, and he went down.

The other man must have realized they weren't alone. He spun around, spotted her and lunged.

Monica dived for the cover of the low wall, but her assailant caught her by the shoulders before she ever reached it. He picked her up, holding her high above the stone floor, before hurling her down again.

Her elbow cracked as she hit the ground, and pain shot through her. Instinctively she crumpled into a ball, clutching her arm, howling as agony surged through her in nauseous waves.

The man kicked her with his boot, rolling her over onto her back before grabbing her. She tried to writhe out of his arms before he could throw her down again. He spun backward, and just as she braced herself for the fall, he seemed to crumple away behind her, and she sagged against a familiar chest.

"Quickly." Thad scooped her up and headed toward the tunnel entrance.

"They'll see us," she protested through the pain.

"I think they're mostly out cold, and we don't have any other choice. We've got to get away." He tucked her feet through the opening and half shoved her through. She shuffled out of his way and scrambled with her good arm to find a flashlight. A moment later he was in the tunnel with her.

Thad clicked on the flashlight and held it in his mouth while he slid the stone cover into place. Then he wrapped her in his arms, carrying her as he started down the stairs.

"Hurry," he panted. "If any of them saw which way we went, they could come after us again any moment."

"I can walk," Monica assured him, flinching when his hand brushed her elbow. "My left arm's useless, but I can walk."

They made their way, half sliding down the steep stairs. Monica was dizzy by the time they reached the bottom. She told herself it was due to the rapid spiraling descent, but she knew the pain radiating up from her arm, combined with lack of sleep, were likely strong contributing factors. And they still had such a long trudge ahead of them.

"We need to hurry." Thad shined the flashlight beam ahead of them.

Monica nodded and lurched forward. Stars danced across her vision as she stood, and she tried to catch her breath, tried to blink back the stars so she could see straight, but the world seemed to be spinning too quickly now, and all she wanted to do was crumple into a ball and rest.

Thad was in her face in an instant. "Monica? Are you okay? Can you keep moving?"

In answer to his questions, she tried to take a step forward, to show him she was fine, but the stars' dance only became that much more frantic, swirling and rushing and threatening at any moment to pull the earth right out from under her feet.

Pinching her eyes shut, she leaned against the wall and propped herself up with her right arm. "Go on without me. You need to get the scepter to safety." She sucked in a ragged breath. "I'll catch up later. I need to rest."

Thad looked at the scepter in his hands and back to Monica. Yes, they needed to get the scepter safely away from Octavian's men, but there had been no sound from above to indicate the men had located the sliding rock that covered the tunnel entrance. The hidden door was in a dark, out-of-the-way corner of the Dorsi fortress. With any luck, even if Octavian's men had spotted which way they went, they'd have great difficulty identifying the panel and figuring out the trick to opening it.

Besides, if the men got the door open and started down the stairs, he and Monica would be able to hear them coming. They already had somewhat of a head start. Their situation wasn't quite as dire as it had been a few minutes before.

He could take a moment for Monica's sake. She'd dug him out of the tunnel and saved his life with her rock throwing. Or at the very least, she'd saved the scepter.

Scooping his arm around her waist, he eased her away from the wall as gently as he could, taking care not to jostle her injured arm. "Monica?" He nuzzled her cheek, and watched her eyes, waiting for a reaction.

Her eyelids fluttered. She winced as she shifted against him, and Thad felt his heart burning inside his chest. For the past six years, he'd stayed far away from her so she wouldn't get hurt. And now she was hurt, in spite of all his sacrifices.

"Monica?" He kissed her cheek lightly.

She moaned.

Guilt tore at him. Earlier, in the car, she'd asked him to share what he was feeling, but he'd pushed her away. Was there any way he could make up for that by sharing with her now?

He could try.

"I never meant for you to get hurt," he began in a whisper.

Instead of snapping at him as she had before, she looked up at him with warmth simmering in her brown eyes.

"All those years when we were friends," he continued, "I never let myself believe I felt anything for you. It wasn't until I was faced with leaving you behind that I realized I couldn't do it. It was selfish of me to marry you so quickly without telling you everything about who I really was, but I didn't know—"

"You didn't know about Octavian."

"I had no idea. I never would have married you, never would have fathered a son if I'd known the risks—"

"Then I'm glad you didn't know."

"Yesterday you said you wished you'd never taken a second look at me."

She looked him up and down, a long, lingering look that melted the last icy corners of his heart. "For the last six years I've wondered where you were, whether you were okay. I've wondered how I could juggle my career and life as a single mother. But I've never once regretted loving you."

Thad drew closer, soaking up the warmth between them. His lips brushed hers.

She lingered for a moment on the edge of his kiss. "I regretted that I couldn't come with you."

A little sob rippled up through her, and Thad pulled her closer, sweeping her into the kiss he'd been holding back for the past six years. She moaned softly, and he realized he hadn't told her half of the truth she deserved to hear.

"When my father explained what Octavian was after, and I realized what I needed to do to stop him, I had two choices. I could run away with you, or run away alone. You loved Seattle. You were looking forward to teaching. You were young and beautiful, and had a promising future. I couldn't ask you to give that up for me. How could I take that from you?" He stroked her hair, which had come loose during her struggle with Octavian's men.

He planted tiny kisses across her temple as he continued. "I was afraid, if I gave you the choice, you would choose me, and then, when it was too late and you'd thrown your future away, you'd wish you hadn't. So I made the choice for you. I went alone, to a place where Octavian would never find me."

Monica kissed him back gently. "I would have gone with you."

"You would have hated it." His lips nipped her nose.

"But we would have been together." She nuzzled him lightly.

Thad felt a pinch of regret. "We can't go back and undo the past."

"What about the future?"

"That depends a lot on what happens with Octavian."

"Does it?"

He wanted to tell her that of course it did, but her question made him pause. He planted anther gentle kiss on her cheek. "I've been telling myself that if I get close to you, Octavian will use my feelings against me. I've been afraid to allow myself to feel what I already feel, because he could use that to hurt us."

When he paused, Monica asked quietly, "What *do* you feel?"

"I feel afraid."

"Of what?"

"Of losing you again. Of losing Peter before I've even had a chance to get to know him, and then losing your love because I'm the one who endangered our son. I'm the one who couldn't keep Octavian away from him."

Monica was quiet for a very long time. Finally, as though she'd thought it over for some time and reached a conclusion, she lifted her face just high enough so that she could see into his eyes. "Don't sacrifice the present for a future that may never come. When you do that, Octavian wins twice."

Then, almost as if she didn't want to face him after speaking her mind, she struggled to her feet. "We should get going."

The brief rest must have been enough to clear her head, because Thad quickly realized he was going to have to hurry to keep up with his wife. As they plodded along in silence, Thad contemplated what Monica had said.

He'd given up six years in hopes of keeping Octavian at bay, but while he'd been hiding out, his enemy had been plotting and conspiring, endangering the very loved ones Thad had gone into hiding to protect. Thad had given up six years—missing out on his son's birth and early childhood—all to avoid a scenario that had ended up happening anyway.

Running away hadn't helped.

His body ached from his battle with Octavian's men. His legs were sore from running, and he was exhausted. With each painful footfall, Thad's determination grew.

He wasn't going to run away again. In fact, he wasn't going to let Octavian get away at all this time. It wasn't enough just to hope that somehow he might get his son back. He *had* to get his son back. And then he'd make certain all of Octavian's schemes were ended for good.

When they reached the pile of crumbling rocks where he'd been nearly buried earlier, Thad and Monica stopped and drank the rest of the bottled water.

"How's your arm?" he asked.

"I think it's broken," she admitted. "But I'll need an X-ray to be sure. What time is it?"

Thad pulled out his phone to check the time. It was just after six in the morning. Thad froze. "Wait a second."

"What?"

He tore the battery from the phone, and the screen went dead.

"What did you do that for?"

"I was wondering how Octavian's men found me on the island. I pulled out my phone to check the time. The helicopter arrived within half an hour."

"You think Octavian is using your phone to somehow track your movements?"

"I don't know. But you asked how his plane found us in Alaska—I had my phone on me then, too. He may have tapped into the satellite system to follow me. Petrela said Octavian always seems to know where people are. Don't phones have some kind of GPS inside them?"

"But how would he access that information?"

Thad thought about the satellite that he'd seen in the sky. He stuffed the dead phone back into his pocket. "He has his ways. Never underestimate Octavian."

He picked up the scepter from where he'd placed it on the pile of rocks, and Monica reached toward it almost reverently before withdrawing her hand, as though unsure whether she was allowed to touch it.

"It's okay." He handed it to her. "Take a look."

"This is the thing everyone's been willing to kill and die for?" She examined it with wide eyes. "It's beautiful, but still..."

"It's not the scepter, but the symbolism behind it and the authority of the document inside."

"Is it waterproof?" she asked, then blushed. "I don't suppose it matters, but when you were outnumbered on the island, I thought perhaps you should throw it into the sea. But the water would get inside and ruin the paper, wouldn't it?"

"It was made well over a thousand years ago, long before waterproof technology," Thad answered, then emitted a sigh that was almost a chuckle. "But come to think of it, I believe we put the document in a plastic zipper bag the last time we had it out."

Monica let out a laugh. "The most precious document in Lydia, stored inside a zipper bag." She handed the scepter back to him.

"The most precious relic in Lydia." Thad rolled the scepter over in his hands. "I had dreamed one day of passing it along to my son."

"Peter would love to be king."

Startled, Thad recalled they'd been interrupted when she was relating what their son knew about him. They'd never gotten around to finishing that conversation. "What have you told him about me?"

"Nothing about the king part—I didn't think that would be wise, in light of your instructions to tell no one of our association with you. I wouldn't want the details leaking out during playgroup." She shook her head. "But about *you?* Yes, Peter knows all about you. He's got your picture by his bed, you know. He prays for you every night before he goes to sleep."

Thad suddenly found it difficult to speak. "What does he pray?"

"That God would watch over you. That he'd get to meet you someday." Her voice went soft, and unshed tears twinkled in her eyes. "I wish you would have told me who you were before we married. You were hiding from me even then. Not on the edge of the earth, but you were hiding part of yourself from me."

Her depth of understanding frightened him, but the lack of condemnation in her voice frightened him even more, twinkling like a glimmer of hope in the darkness. He'd moved his face closer to hers, and now placed a gentle kiss on her forehead. "You were happy without me."

"For Peter's sake I told myself to be happy, but I missed you." A tear dropped from her cheek to the dry stones.

Thad watched it fall. His throat felt thick. He pulled Monica against him gently, taking care with her arm. "I missed you, too. So much. I missed out on Peter's childhood. He doesn't know me."

Monica met his eyes in the dim glimmer of the flashlight's beam. "Peter loves you."

"He doesn't know me," Thad repeated.

"True. But he loves you just the same."

"I suppose he'll only be disappointed once he meets me."

"No. He'll only be disappointed if you run away again."

Thad stayed silent for a long time. It hurt to hear what Monica had to say, but she'd earned the right to say it, and he knew he deserved to hear it. Like picking at a healing scab, curiosity drove him to prod further. "I thought if I hid myself from you, then you wouldn't truly know me, and it wouldn't really hurt when you left."

He sucked in a ragged breath, still marveling that after six years he could finally hold her in his arms. "Not only did I suffer the pain of our separation, but I've spent the last six years regretting that I had never fully shared my secrets with you. All those years we were friends, even during our whirlwind romance, I was never fully there."

"You were already in hiding." Monica rose shakily to her feet, favoring her injured arm. "You're in hiding still."

Thad stood beside her. "I don't want to hide anymore."

Her eyes fell on the scepter, and he looked at it, too, tightening his grip around the staff. They still had a journey ahead of them. They still had to get Peter back from Octavian, and keep Lydia from the madman's grasp. And he had no idea how they were going to accomplish it.

"I'm tired. It's already morning. We should get moving," Monica whispered.

Thad nodded and plodded after her, the scepter in his hand weighing him down almost as much as the heaviness in his heart. He wanted to hold Monica and never let her go. But before he could do that, he had to get Peter back.

They found his siblings gathering in the family dining room for breakfast. To Thad's surprise, an older couple sat among them, leaping up the moment Monica entered the room.

"Mom? Dad?" Monica's mouth dropped, but as she stumbled toward them her smile grew. "How did you get here?"

"We took a flight the moment you said our grandson's disappearance had to do with all the news you'd been watching about the upheaval in the kingdom of Lydia," Richard Miller pronounced, scowling at Thad as he leaned toward his wife. "You're right, darling. The picture on Peter's nightstand does bear remarkable resemblance to the missing Lydian prince."

"Are you all right?" Sheila Miller reached toward Monica with open arms, but stepped back when her daughter grabbed her broken arm and winced.

"My arm—" she looked at her father, who was a doctor "—I think it may be broken."

"Then we'll have to get you to a hospital," Richard Miller stated with authority, casting a stern look at Thad.

For a moment, Thad thought about apologizing for leaving Monica alone and pregnant so many years before and for the connections that had resulted in Peter's kidnapping. The fact that her arm was likely broken didn't help matters. But Monica's parents appeared as though they were ready to take her to the hospital that very moment, and Thad knew a proper apology would take time, as would proper introductions.

"Shall we head for the hospital now?" Richard asked Monica.

"Yes. We need to hurry so I can get back here." She looked at Thad, her eyes brimming with understanding and—could it be?—love. If that's what he saw there, he knew he didn't deserve it.

He brushed a gentle kiss across her forehead as she stepped past him.

Thad handed over the scepter to his brother.

Alec gave him a wry smile. "I was shot and tortured for this." He rolled it between his hands, inspecting the crown-shaped head.

"Keep it safe." Ravenous, Thad peeled a banana

and took a bite. "Has anything happened while I was gone?"

Levi cleared his throat. "My father's been looking into Octavian's holdings. He forwarded me a list of some of the companies Octavian controls."

Thad took the sheaf of papers from his sister's fiancé and flipped through them, spotting the name of his satellite phone provider. He shared his suspicions with the others. "Octavian's men caught up to me the moment I got my hands on the scepter. I figured he must have tracked me through my phone, but I didn't know how."

"If he owns the satellites, which it appears he does, he could follow your phone with tremendous precision," Levi confirmed.

"I've taken the battery out. Will that stop him?"

"It should."

"That's something, at least. What time is it?"

"Nearly seven o'clock." Stasi consulted a bracelet-style watch on her wrist. "We have just over five hours until the exchange. Why don't you go take a shower? You look terrible."

Thad caught his reflection in a mirror hanging on the opposite wall. His sister was right. He didn't want his little boy to see him for the first time looking like this. Peter was already likely to be frightened enough. "I'll take a quick shower and change clothes. Then I want to meet back here."

"To plot our strategy?" Alec clarified.

"Yes." Thad swallowed. He'd told Monica he was tired of hiding—from her, and from God. "And to pray."

Monica fought against the heavy veil of sleep. She needed to protect Peter. She needed to support Thad. There wasn't time for rest. Granted, they'd put her under while they reset the bone in her arm, but she'd roused enough to drink a sip of something fruity her mother had held for her. Surely an hour or more had passed. She needed to get back to the palace. She couldn't be late.

What was happening now?

Opening her eyes with effort, Monica looked around the small recovery room for any sign of her parents. Where were they?

Had they left her? They wouldn't leave her alone—not unless something more important had come up. But what could be more important at this point? Only the exchange with Octavian, but that wasn't until noon.

Wait—what if it *was* noon already? She'd told her parents of all that had happened, and stressed the importance of getting back to the palace well ahead of noon. Surely her parents hadn't left her to rest and miss the exchange!

A jolt of fear shot through her, and she opened her eyes wide.

There was someone in her room after all. With

effort, Monica managed to turn her head slightly to one side. The broad-shouldered figure reminded her of Thad, but she quickly realized it wasn't him.

"General Petrela?" Her voice sounded surprisingly weak.

He'd brought a wheelchair in and parked it next to her bed. "I told you earlier you need to trust me. We have to go."

"Without my parents? Where are they? Where are we going?"

Suddenly he reached for her, and she instinctively pulled away, but his arms encircled her in spite of her feeble resistance. Was he trying to kidnap her?

"You had the chance to come nicely. I don't have time to explain."

Still groggy, Monica pushed at him, and tried to protest, but the general covered her mouth with a scented cloth like the one her kidnappers had used when they'd taken her during her morning run. No! She held her breath and tried to fight, to cry out, to stop him from taking her away. Then she choked on her breath and everything went dark again.

ELEVEN

"Have you seen Monica? Do you know where she is?"

Interrupted in the midst of his prayer time with his family, Thad's already-exhausted mind was slow to identify the caller. The voice was familiar...Richard Miller, and he sounded frantic.

"I thought she was with you, at the hospital." Thad pulled Stasi's arm close and squinted at the delicate numbers on her watch. They had less than two hours before Octavian's arrival. He'd expected Monica to return anytime.

"Sheila and I were at her bedside when a nurse brought us a note from your mother. It said your father was awake and wanted to speak with us."

"What?" Thad felt his blood run cold.

"But he wasn't. He's still in a coma, though his vital signs are improving. I'm afraid the note was a ruse to get us away from Monica."

His head spinning from the sudden rush of fear,

Thad tried to piece together what Richard was saying. "Monica is missing?"

"When we returned to her room, she was gone."

Sheila Miller's voice cut in. "But her shoes were still there. She wouldn't have gone far barefoot."

"Not on her own," Thad acknowledged, quickly surmising what had happened. When Octavian's men failed to take the scepter the night before, Octavian would have felt the loss and wanted a stronger bargaining position. His men could have easily guessed that Monica had been injured.

And Octavian had connections at the hospital—or at the very least, Lucca had. Thad wished he'd thought to send some of his father's guards to watch over Monica's room, but he'd been too exhausted to think. He'd assumed she was safe with her parents. Too late, he realized he'd never even briefed them on the situation. He'd been too ashamed to face them. With regret, he realized part of him was still trying to hide.

"Keep looking for her. I can dispatch security to scour the hospital." Thad winced at the thought of losing more manpower at the worst possible time. He needed every man he had to cover the palace.

"I really don't think we're going to find her here."

Thad groaned as his heart began to mourn for Monica. Why had he let her out of his sight? "Come on back to the palace, then. We've only got a couple of hours."

As he closed the call, a wave of despair passed over him, and he pinched his eyes shut. In spite of all his efforts to remain emotionally detached, he'd allowed himself to fall right back in love with Monica, to hope against all hope that somehow, things might work out between them.

Arms wrapped around him, and he opened his eyes to see his siblings surrounding him.

"Monica's been kidnapped?" Isabelle clarified.

Thad tried to answer, but his nodding head sagged against the arms that supported him, and he felt his anger and despair rising up with the hot tears that flooded his eyes. He clutched the scepter, realizing that, for all his efforts to retrieve it, he still hadn't saved his family. Octavian had both Monica and Peter now.

"Dear God, we ask for Your guidance and strength." Alec's deep voice rumbled beside him, and his sisters and their fiancés joined in, their voices blended in chorus as each of them poured out their hearts for the welfare of his wife and son.

Though it exposed his deepest fears and the parts of his heart he'd tried hardest to hide, Thad forced his lips to utter honest words as he whispered a plea to God.

"Mommy, wake up. Mommy?"

Monica rolled over, away from the nudge against her shoulder.

"Mommy, wake up."

"Mmm." She pinched her eyes shut. "Do you want pancakes or waffles for breakfast?"

"Mommy!" Peter's voice sounded incredulous. "You can't make waffles here."

Suddenly Monica remembered, and sat bolt upright. She wasn't at home in Seattle. It wasn't a lazy summer morning. Her world had been upended, her son kidnapped, and now she was with him again. She'd been kidnapped, too.

She pulled him into her arms and covered his head with kisses. "Peter! Are you okay? I'm so glad to see you, I missed you so much!"

Peter basked for a moment in her attention, then batted away her kisses. "I'm okay, Mommy. Natalie has been watching me. We flew in a plane and we got to go to the beach!"

"The beach." Monica felt the fear-wedged tension leave her body like a sigh. Her little boy hadn't been terrified. He'd missed her, but he'd been enjoying the beach and the plane ride. And he trusted his favorite babysitter, a standout student in the foreign languages department where Monica taught. "Where is Natalie?"

"Out here." Peter led her out of the room where she'd been sleeping, to a comfortable-looking, carpeted living room, where an elaborate train set filled most of one end of the room, a stack of children's books teetered near the sofa, and a large-screen television with a home entertainment system occupied most of one wall, its screen dark.

Monica smiled. Natalie knew Peter wasn't supposed to watch more than a half hour of television. The babysitter jumped up from the couch the moment she spotted Monica.

"Let me show you what my train does!" Peter leaped at the toy and quickly got to work setting the pieces where he wanted them.

"Okay, you show me." Monica knew it might take her son several minutes before he was ready to give his train presentation. She turned to Natalie, whose eyes were wide with fright.

"What's happened, Professor Miller? Strange men gave me a note written in Old Lydian. They said it was from you. The note claimed you'd been injured and needed me to bring Peter to you, but I didn't expect we'd be leaving the country." She looked at the cast on Monica's arm. "You *were* injured. But what are we doing halfway around the world, and who is the creepy guy with the orange face?"

"Octavian?" Monica got a word in when her frantic student paused to breathe. "He can't be trusted."

Her words seemed to confirm Natalie's fears. "I should have stopped to think. Peter was at your parents' house. But you're the only person I know who knows Old Lydian, so I thought the note must really be from you. And I was so worried when they said you were hurt, all I could think of was getting

Peter to you quickly, and keeping him from being frightened." Her voice cracked, and she wiped a tear away quickly as though Peter might see.

"Natalie." Monica patted her shoulder, regretfully realizing Octavian would have had no trouble spotting the connection between Peter and Natalie. The babysitter was often at their house. And Natalie's dissertation project, comparing Old Lydian with Ancient Greek, had recently been featured on the department website. "You didn't know. I probably would have fallen for an Old Lydian note, too. I'm glad you kept Peter from getting scared."

Natalie sniffled and glanced at Peter, who was absorbed in playing with the train. The babysitter leaned a little closer to Monica and spoke quietly, her voice still trembling. "What *is* going on? I think we're being held prisoner, and I'm pretty sure we're somewhere off the coast of Greece, but I can't begin to imagine *why*."

In between clapping for Peter and encouraging him in his game, Monica explained to Natalie the situation with Octavian, her history with Thaddeus and the impending showdown that was rapidly approaching.

Natalie's eyes grew wider and wider behind her glasses as she absorbed everything Monica said, asking clarifying questions at some of the more confusing parts. She pulled an album from the stack of books near the sofa.

"So, this is Octavian." She pointed to a picture of the man, heavily airbrushed to make him look better.

"Yes."

"We've met him a few times. He's seemed quite eager to make a favorable impression on Peter. He gave him the train set and lots of other toys. He told me to show him this album—the captions make all these men sound like heroes."

Monica absorbed the news without surprise. "He's already trying to win him over so he can control him. He wants Peter to admire him and his coconspirators." The thought made her feel sick to her stomach. Octavian was essentially trying to brainwash her impressionable young son.

Natalie flipped through the album to another page. "Who's this guy?"

"General Marc Petrela." At the sight of the man's picture, Monica recalled the way he'd abruptly pulled her from the hospital, and the memory doused her with a fresh wave of fear. She'd been so relieved to see Peter safe and sound, she'd lost track of time. "Why do you ask?"

Natalie's eyes narrowed and her voice dropped to a faint whisper, while she quickly flipped the album to a random page, almost as though she was afraid someone might see the picture and guess who she was talking about. "He said some things—" She shook her head. "I didn't understand what he was getting at, but it makes more sense now that you've told me the rest of what's been going on."

"What did he say?" Monica felt her pulse rate rise. She'd long been wondering whether Petrela could be trusted. Since he'd kidnapped her from the hospital, she was ready to believe he was working for Octavian and had no intention of helping Thad and his family regain the crown, but she was eager to hear what Natalie had to say.

"I think he was trying to warn me not to trust Octavian. He said he wanted me to pass Peter to him during the exchange, that he'd—" She squinted, clearly trying to recall the precise words the man had used. "He said he'd *cover* him. What does that mean?"

"The exchange." Monica had kept her eyes open for a clock since she'd entered the room, but had seen no sign of one. "What time is it? Saturday at noon, Octavian is planning to meet at the palace throne room, to exchange Peter for the scepter. And today is Saturday."

"It's got to be nearly noon now. They took my phone when we boarded the plane and I haven't seen it since, but the sun is rising high in the sky."

"Then we should be leaving soon." Monica swallowed back her fear. Was Octavian going to keep his promise to exchange Peter for the scepter, or had everything he'd said been a lie? And even if the madman followed through and handed Peter over to Thaddeus, what would become of *her?*

Thad opened the conference room cabinet that held the whiteboard, grabbed a marker and drew a line down the middle. They had just over an hour before Octavian arrived.

Kirk had brought in the newly appointed head of the royal guard, a man named Jason, as well as his right-hand man, Linus. Alec brought in his most trusted men from the army, Titus and Julian, and they worked together with the guard officials to position their men to defend the throne room, as well as the palace itself.

"We'll have all entrances and exits covered ten men deep. No one will get in or out of the palace without our permission," Alec assured his brother.

"If your wife and son arrive with Octavian, we won't let them leave again," Kirk assured him.

Thad wanted to believe it would be that easy. He prayed that Peter and Monica would be all right. More than that, he begged God to give him a second chance.

But now, alone with just his brother and sisters, their fiancés and Dom Procopio, Thad couldn't stand still. He was determined to make every possible preparation in hopes of keeping Peter and Monica safe.

He labeled one column on the whiteboard *Octavian,* and the other *Us*.

"He's got Peter and Monica." Thad filled in the empty space under his enemy's name, writing quickly. "He's got billions of dollars in resources, a mercenary army, unknown intel and six years' head start in planning this thing." Thad blew out a long breath and looked around the table. "What have we got?"

"The scepter." Alexander held out the object he'd vowed to protect with his life.

Thad prayed it wouldn't come to that.

"We have the home turf advantage," Levi noted.

"But he picked the spot," Isabelle reminded them, "so I wonder how much of an advantage that will end up being. I can't help but suspect he has a reason for wanting to meet here. As Petrela pointed out, Octavian had the run of the place for almost a week while we were in hiding, and we know he had devices brought in. They may have been listening devices, or he could have rigged an ambush. He could have done anything."

"We've scoured the palace, and it appears to be undisturbed," Stasi noted. "But I agree. We can't assume he hasn't done something to make our advantage his."

Thad had already written *turf* in their column, but he put a question mark after the word. "Anything else?" Their column looked woefully small and uncertain compared to Octavian's advantages.

"We've got the royal guard," Kirk offered.

"And the army," Alexander added. "Insofar as they'll answer to me." Having only been appointed head general the week before, he'd hardly had an opportunity to alert his men of the change, let alone establish any protocol.

"They'll answer to you." Lily squeezed his hand.

"But what about Petrela?" Alec asked. "He's disappeared again, and we still don't know with any certainty where he stands."

Thad's pen hovered over the column line. Then he reluctantly wrote *Petrela* in Octavian's column. "Anything else?"

He looked around the room, but didn't hear a response, and started to put the cap back on his marker.

"Your Majesty?" Dom Procopio cleared his throat. "You have God on your side."

Thad felt a shameful blush creeping up his neck. "I haven't always been faithful," he admitted, shaking his head. "I was mad at God for letting Lydia fall into this situation in the first place. I was angry that God forced me out of my homeland and my marriage. I've returned to my faith in God. I want to hope He'll see us through, but—" he gave the lopsided columns a long look "—it's hard to have hope when my wife and son are in the hands of someone so evil."

"I don't believe God intends for Octavian to control them," Dom Procopio told him bluntly.

When Thad looked up, he saw that Lillian Bardici had raised her hand.

"Yes?"

She looked sheepish as she started to speak. "When your brother and I were trudging through the desert without water, I thought we were going to die. I really did. But we kept walking anyway, and now we're here, and we're engaged." She squeezed the prince's hand. "Sometimes what looks like the end is really just the beginning."

Thad wasn't sure what to make of her story.

His brother met his eyes. "Soldier on."

Monica wasn't sure what to expect. But then, she figured that was likely part of Octavian's strategy. If her attention was focused on sorting out what was going on, she'd have less time to figure out a means of escaping. Besides, why should he tell her anything? She was a pawn. And he was playing for the crown.

But even though she didn't know what to expect, she felt her son deserved some warning about what was about to unfold. Without her purse or phone, she had no pictures of Thad to show him. She pulled

Peter onto her lap and asked, "Do you remember the picture that sits by your bed?"

"Of Daddy?"

"That's the one. Do you know where Mommy has been for the last few days?"

"On a trip."

"That's right." Her son had answered with the exact explanation she'd given her parents before she'd left. "I went on a trip to look for your daddy."

His eyes flashed with excitement and he bounced on her lap. "Did you find him?"

Sudden emotion swelled her throat, taking her by surprise. She'd thought she had a handle on the situation, but she hadn't realized until she'd seen the sparkle in Peter's eyes—so like Thad's eyes—how emotionally raw she still felt.

She still had feelings for Thad. Strong feelings. But she couldn't let those feelings get the best of her. She had to keep a clear head. Octavian already had too many advantages.

"Yes," she answered in a whisper, "I found your daddy. He looks a lot like the picture by your bed, but his hair is longer now. I'd forgotten how tall he was. He's the tallest person in the room, no matter where he is."

Peter looked at her expectantly, his eager expression just like the look he always got on his face just before opening a present. Monica worked up the courage to tell him the rest of what she knew he needed to know. "Your father loves you very much. We're going to try to visit him."

"Yay!" Peter nearly leaped off her lap.

She had to shush him. "Listen, Peter, this is important. You remember that man who gave you the train set?"

"Octo-man?"

"Octavian." Monica pronounced the name patiently. "Octavian wants you to think he's nice, but he's not. He's the reason you haven't been able to see your daddy all this time. And, Peter?"

Her son nodded solemnly, absorbing the news about the father he'd wanted to meet for so long.

"If anything happens to me, I need you to know that you can trust your daddy. You can't trust Octavian. He's not a nice man. He might try to tell you things about your father that aren't true. He might even try to tell you that I don't love you. But you know I love you, right?"

"I know," Peter whispered. "I love you."

Tears dripped down Monica's nose, but she swept them away. She had to keep herself together. "Your father loves you, too. If you ever have to choose between Octavian or Daddy, choose your father, okay?"

"Okay." Peter threw his arms around her neck. "But I want to choose you, too." Then he looked at her with earnest blue-green eyes. "Is that okay? Can I choose you *and* Daddy?"

Monica struggled to speak calmly and clearly, though her heart felt as though it might burst. "I hope so, Peter. I hope you can choose us both."

Peter snuggled on her lap awhile longer, content just to be near her after being apart for so long. Then someone knocked on the door.

"Come in."

She'd half expected Octavian, but it was General Petrela. Though she wanted to cling to the sliver of hope that Petrela might be working for the Royal House of Lydia, as he'd claimed, Monica immediately realized Petrela would be foolish to try to cross Octavian. Could he have possibly operated right under the egomaniac's nose for so long? Petrela was the only one of the three conspiring generals still living. Surely he hadn't survived so long while planning to double-cross his boss.

She'd have to watch him carefully. And for now, she'd have to do whatever he said.

"Please come with me."

Monica scooped up Peter and carried him tightly in her arms as she followed the general. They'd provided her with shoes and fresh clothing, just as they had for Peter, but the brand-new sneakers squeaked as she walked down the long hallway to the exterior doors.

The blades of the helicopter were already moving when they stepped outside. Peter looked excited about the opportunity to ride on a helicopter, though he balked slightly when they approached the craft.

"It's going to be okay," Monica whispered, and Peter relaxed. She hoped she was right.

TWELVE

There was nothing left to do but wait.

Thad checked the lines of communication one more time. The men posted at all the doors responded in a timely manner, as did those stationed at all the major hallways inside the palace.

Even the first-floor windows were all guarded.

Still Thad couldn't suppress the sickly feeling inside his stomach. It didn't matter how tight a lid they kept on the building. If Thad had to choose between letting Octavian harm his wife or son, and watching him walk away, he'd choose the latter.

As he looked around the circle at his brother and sisters, he couldn't help but be in awe of the love each of them had found. Though the future of their kingdom remained uncertain, they each had someone who would love and support them through the trials ahead, who made them smile even in the midst of hardship. Six years before, when he was young and afraid, he'd turned his back on such a love.

They went around the circle and each person

prayed. Then it was Thad's turn. He asked God to protect his kingdom and keep his people safe. He prayed that the sacrifices his siblings and their friends had made would not be in vain. And then his voice creaked as he dared to ask for something he was certain he didn't deserve.

"Dear God, if You could see fit to give me back my family..." His voice broke, and he realized there wasn't any way he could continue. He'd willingly walked away from his wife, but it had been a mistake. Now he wondered if he'd ever get the chance to tell her he still loved her.

A hoarse-voiced chorus of "Amen" closed the prayer, and his sisters hugged him before running off to the balcony that overlooked the throne room, the safest place he knew of for them to watch the meeting with Octavian.

And they'd insisted on watching.

Alec approached him, scepter in hand. "I believe this belongs to you."

Thad couldn't help recalling the solemn way his father had handed it over eight years before, when Thad had signed his name, promising to lead the tiny kingdom faithfully.

He was ready to be faithful to God again. But would God deem him worthy of ruling? He didn't feel worthy.

"No one's ever asked the question of what you

should do if Octavian forces you to choose between the scepter, or your wife and son."

"I have to defend the scepter at all costs. You were shot for it."

"I couldn't have given it away if I'd wanted to. I didn't know where it was." Alec gave Thad a stern look. "It's just a hollow hunk of metal."

"But it signifies—"

"It signifies that the man who holds it is God's chosen ruler of Lydia. I don't believe God would choose a leader who would hand over his wife or son in exchange for a hollow hunk of metal."

Thad swallowed. He understood. "But if Octavian gets his hands on the scepter—"

Alec had already started to walk away. "Sometimes what looks like the end is really the beginning."

Monica glanced up several times at the stoic general who shared the helicopter with them. If there was any chance he was on their side, she wanted to give him ample opportunity to communicate his plan, using eyebrow twitches if necessary, since Octavian was facing them both, his silent glare as terrifying as any of the threats he'd previously spoken.

Petrela didn't twitch. Not even his eyebrows. He sat stiffly in place, and Monica slowly realized he was wearing thick body armor under his uniform. She glanced at Octavian, and surmised that he was similarly protected. Suddenly she felt even more vulnerable, and hugged Peter close, as though her embrace could shield him as effectively as the armor the men wore.

What was it Petrela had told Natalie? Something about covering Peter?

Fear traced its cold finger down her spine. These men were going in expecting something, weren't they? And they didn't care what happened to her.

Thankfully, Peter was content to watch the Lydian shoreline pass by beneath them. He didn't bounce around excitedly as she might have expected him to on a helicopter ride. But then, there was a stress-filled vibe in the air that, even at five years of age, Peter likely felt strongly enough that it kept him glued to his seat.

"Look at that castle, Mommy," he whispered, more excited about the palace turrets than any other landmark they'd passed.

"I think that's where we're going."

"Are we? Do you think there's a king who lives there?"

Monica swallowed back the emotion that surged upward at his innocent question. "Yes," she answered softly, "a very good and noble king." Though she'd criticized him for hiding, Monica realized Thad had acted nobly. She wanted to apologize for her harsh words. But she had to survive the exchange first.

The helicopter settled down in the courtyard, and they stepped out to find themselves surrounded by guards.

Octavian didn't appear to be the least bit surprised by the guards. He was vastly outnumbered, arriving, as he had, with only two guards, plus the general. Monica looked around, half expecting to see Octavian's mercenaries appear from out of the sky, but all she saw were royal guards.

What was the man up to? He strode confidently into the palace, and Petrela motioned for her to follow. Peter wanted to walk, so Monica set him down, but kept tight hold of his hand. She followed Octavian and his guards down the hallway with Petrela following her.

She'd seen enough of Octavian's mercenaries to know the man could have brought in enough forces to outnumber Thad's armies two to one.

And yet, he'd come alone.

Why?

As they entered the throne room and Monica saw all the men the royal family had stationed there, she felt the imbalance all the more acutely. Considering the stakes, Octavian wouldn't have let himself be outnumbered so vastly unless he had a very good reason for doing so.

Monica feared the reality was more accurately a very *evil* reason.

* * *

Thad's breath caught in his throat as Monica's familiar figure stepped into the room, nearly overshadowed by Octavian, Petrela and the two guards with him. Their party shifted formation as they came through the doorway, and Thad spotted a golden-haired boy holding Monica's hand. Thad's heart caught in his throat. He'd never seen anything that moved him as much as the sight of his wife and son.

"Peter." The name left Thad's lips in a silent whisper, and he felt the challenge of all that lay ahead. He would keep this little boy safe.

Peter's blue-green eyes roved the room, wide with wonder as he took in the high-lofted ceiling, the heavy inlaid thrones and the crown in its glass case near the front of the room.

"Wow." His cherub lips hung open in awe, and he tugged on his mother's arm.

She bent slightly, and they exchanged whispers. Thad wished he could hear what they said, but when Monica pointed his way he knew.

Peter's gaze followed his mother's hand until he saw him, and a bright grin lit up his face.

Thad wanted to smile a greeting, to do something to communicate his love and support to the boy, but his sorrow and concern were too great. He'd already been such a disappointment as a father—

absent, completely absent. He'd endangered his son. He endangered him still.

But Peter didn't look disappointed. His wide eyes twinkled and he looked as though he might have gone running forward, had his mother not kept a tight hold on him, tugging him back against her and crossing her arms over his chest. They stood no more than three meters away from him, and yet Thad felt as though the gulf between them was immeasurable.

Octavian stepped forward, stealing Thad's attention away from Peter.

"You have the scepter." His plasticized face was expressionless. "I have a document that requires your signature." Octavian walked over to a side table. "You will sign here in exchange for your wife."

"What about my son?"

"When this transaction is complete, you will hand over the scepter, and *then* I will give you back your son."

Two for two. It made sense. Octavian had been unable to steal the scepter out from under him, so he'd taken his wife instead. He needed two things to reign: Thad's signature and the scepter. He'd trade his wife and son, one for each. It was mathematically sound.

But Thad didn't like the terms at all.

And Octavian didn't seem to like waiting. "You

will comply with my request, or we will leave, and you will never see your wife and son again."

Thad crossed his arms over his chest. "I need to know why you think you have grounds to make these demands."

"I made a deal with your father. He tried to back out of it. I'm just doing what I must to claim what's rightfully mine."

"According to *you*. I've never seen any proof that my father ever agreed to anything beyond the business arrangements that have been fulfilled in the past."

Octavian's eyeballs bulged, and he raised one gloved hand, pointing his index finger up toward the high vaulted ceiling. "I have been wronged by your family—"

But before Octavian finished his sentence, another voice carried through the room. "No, Octavian. You have wronged my family."

Thad spun around at the sound of his father's weak but unmistakable voice.

Queen Elaine had entered the throne room from one of the back hallways, pushing the former King Philip in a wheelchair.

Philip continued, "My family owes you nothing. Lydia owes you nothing." He turned to face Thad. "Son, if you will open the scepter, you will find inside the key that opens the file drawer under the display case of the crown. There you will find a record of every agreement I ever made with Octavian, including the history of his royal titles, which I now hereby denounce on grounds of treason."

Octavian stiffened visibly. His upraised, gloved hand twitched as he lowered his index finger. His hand now stabbed skyward like a fist. "I have your wife and son." He addressed Thad. "If you wish to be held liable for their deaths, by all means, unlock the drawer. If you wish to have your wife and son returned to you, sign the document and *hand over the scepter!*"

Thad hesitated. His father's arrival had tipped the tables, but the upset only appeared to have made Octavian that much more desperate. Thad looked over and met Monica's eyes. "What do you think I should do?" he asked aloud.

"I think—" She licked her lips nervously and dipped her head as though she wanted to speak with him alone and not be overheard by anyone else. But the room was too large and crowded for that to happen. Nonetheless, she lowered her voice. "You should have your family and your men clear the room."

Her request seemed odd. He hadn't expected such a specific response. And yet, as he took a step back, he realized the two guards who'd come in with Octavian were fiddling with something.

Not guns.

He couldn't see clearly what the men had, but he

felt the warning Monica had been trying to send. Octavian's upraised fist shifted. He extended all four of his fingers.

Thad watched, wondering if the man was counting down, or trying to send some kind of warning.

Then he realized Octavian's message wasn't for him.

It was for the guards who'd come in with him, a preplanned signal for destruction. They didn't have guns. They held something far more deadly.

Detonation devices.

All at once, Thad realized precisely why Octavian had wanted to meet in this particular room. He'd had it rigged while the royal family was ousted. And he had every intention of destroying any evidence that would prove he had no right to the throne.

Thad dived across the table toward Monica and Peter as he screamed, "Clear the room!"

Monica watched the scene unfold as if in slow motion. On the edges of her peripheral vision, she saw the princesses on the balcony above sprint for the safety of the doorways behind them. Elaine whipped Philip's wheelchair around and pushed it toward the back door.

Thad slid across the table toward them, but he couldn't possibly reach them in time. Octavian stood between them. And the heavily armored tyrant didn't seem nearly as concerned about the potential explosives as the rest of the occupants of the room.

Which meant his body armor was likely strong enough to protect him from whatever was about to erupt.

Monica put the facts together quickly. Petrela had told Natalie that he would cover Peter.

At the time, she hadn't understood what he'd meant by his cryptic instructions. Now she guessed that Petrela's armor could withstand the blast—that he could protect Peter.

She plucked up her son and shoved him toward the waiting general's outstretched arms. She didn't know what Petrela intended to do with Peter once the smoke cleared, but at least her son would be protected during the blast.

Petrela gathered Peter in his wide embrace, settling him quickly against the stone floor, covering him as a series of eruptions spewed fire and smoke all around them.

Monica felt someone slam into her. For one disoriented moment, she thought perhaps Thad had gotten past Octavian after all.

But then she realized it *was* Octavian.

He pulled her through the chaos toward a doorway.

She tried to fight him, but the eruptions had her doubled over in a fit of coughing. Whatever had just exploded sent tears to her eyes, stinging her throat.

She stumbled.

Octavian hauled her after him, his grip surprisingly strong, his stride steady as they ducked down the hall. Monica lunged the other way, but before she could break free from his grasp, she felt the cold press of metal against her back. A gun.

"If you want to live to see your son again, you'll come with me."

Still hardly able to talk or breathe, Monica wasn't sure how to respond. She wanted to get away from Octavian, to get back to her husband and son. And yet, she was certain the tyrant behind her had been pushed to the breaking point. He wouldn't hesitate to pull the trigger.

He tugged her around a corner and froze.

Guards barred the way ahead of them.

Octavian cursed.

Monica sensed the man's panic level reaching a critical state. He was surrounded. For a man who hated losing, who'd never given up the tantrums of toddlerhood, a critical state of panic wasn't an option.

The barrel of the gun jabbed deeper under her ribs.

Monica looked back down the hallway and recognized the small storage room that led to the tunnel under the sea.

If she could convince Octavian to escape through the tunnel, maybe he would cool down. She could get away from him later, or Thad could find her. Maybe. Or maybe she'd just end up giving away a national secret that had gone undetected for hundreds of years.

As the smoke cleared in the hallway, the guards ahead of them spun around, spotting them.

"Don't come any closer, or I'll shoot her!" Octavian had sweat dripping in beads down his forehead, sliding in slimy trails off his upper lip.

She heard the thunder of boots up ahead. More guards were coming.

Octavian's grip tightened on her arm. The hand that held the gun twitched more crazily the closer the guards came.

"I can get you out of here," she whispered. "There's a secret passage."

"No. The passage is up ahead." He motioned past the guards. "It leads to the catacombs. I have a helicopter waiting at the other end."

"There's another passage behind us. Let me show you. It leads under the sea."

Octavian hesitated. More guards arrived at the end of the hallway. There was no way Octavian would reach the passage he'd planned for his escape.

He tugged her backward. "Show me the way. But if you try to get away, I'll shoot you."

Thad scrambled through the smoke and flames toward the spot where he'd last seen Monica.

She was gone.

The smoke rose slowly and he sank toward the floor, coughing. The air was clearer lower down, and he could just make out a tangle of arms and legs ahead of him. The man's uniform looked familiar.

Struggling to breathe in the poisoned air, Thad crawled across the floor to the figures.

"Petrela," he sputtered against the burn in his lungs.

The man rose slowly, revealing the child he'd held protected against the floor. "Your son, Your Majesty." The general lifted Peter to standing, handing him over freely.

Peter rose shakily to his knees. Already the smoke had begun to dissipate through the lofty room, and Thad was breathing easier. He heard the spurting of fire extinguishers around him as the guards put out the small blazes that had erupted. Thad was nearly certain Octavian had only meant to create enough of a diversion to allow himself an opportunity to get away—not enough to risk any injury to himself.

If he'd meant for them to be killed, they would have been.

"Daddy?" Peter smiled uncertainly.

"Yes." Thad crawled closer and scooped the little boy onto his lap.

Peter looked at him warily. "Where's Mommy?"

Thad looked around. Most of the people had

cleared out of the room, except for the guards who'd extinguished the flames. He saw no sign of Monica.

Petrela shook his head. "Octavian took her. He was planning to get away through a secret passage. I can show you the way."

As they rose to their feet, Alec trotted over as quickly as his orthopedic brace would allow. "All my men have checked in. The exits are secure. Octavian hasn't left the building."

"Show us the passageway," Thad instructed Petrela. He carried Peter in his arms, the little boy clinging to him as he ran after the general down the hallway. A crowd of guards filled the corridor.

Thad recognized Linus, one of Kirk's trusted friends. "Did Octavian come this way?"

The guard nodded apologetically. "He was holding Monica hostage. I couldn't allow my men to advance—the man was desperate. He was ready to pull the trigger."

"They got no farther down the hall?" Petrela clarified.

"They retreated back this way." The guard pointed. "By the time we came around the corner, they'd disappeared. We can't find them anywhere."

"Where could they go from there?" Petrela asked.

Thad looked at the general. He wasn't sure how much he should trust a man who'd worked closely with Octavian, but Petrela had kept Peter safe and handed him over, even though he'd had ample opportunity to escape with the heir in the confusion.

Petrela seemed to sense Thad's wariness. "I've been collecting evidence against Octavian for the last five years. We can put him away on a hundred different charges, but we have to find him first." He pointed past the guards. "The entrance to the secret passage is that way. If he didn't get past these guards, he couldn't have used it." Petrela looked at Alec and Kirk, who'd been checking in with their men.

"No one else has seen any sign of him," Kirk confirmed. "All the exits are covered."

"Then he's got to be somewhere in the palace," Alec concluded.

Thad felt his shoulders droop. The palace had more than a hundred rooms. Searching it could take forever. "Keep your men posted at all the exits and windows," Thad instructed Alec and Kirk. "Have the rest of your troops do a thorough search."

Isabelle and Levi ran up behind them.

"Where's Monica?" Isabelle asked.

As Kirk and Alec dispersed to instruct their men, Thad hugged Peter to his chest and explained, "Octavian took her. They've got to be somewhere in the building. We have reason to believe Octavian knows about some of the secret passages."

"There are hundreds of places to hide in the palace," Isabelle moaned.

"Your father has a map of the passages," Levi reminded her. "We can take a look and start searching."

"It's not an exhaustive map," Thad acknowledged, "but it's an excellent place to start. You two get on that."

As the pair ran off down the hall hand in hand, Peter whimpered, "Mommy's missing?"

"Yes." Thad tried not to let his regret overwhelm him. His son was in his arms, and he still held the scepter tight in one hand. Octavian hadn't won.

Not yet, anyway.

THIRTEEN

"We should pray for Mommy," Peter whispered.

Thad swallowed past the lump in his throat. "Yes," he agreed. "We should." He wasted no time launching into a murmured prayer, his eyes pinched shut as he begged God to protect Monica and help them find her.

Peter surprised him by joining in without hesitation. "Help us find Mommy. And make it so my daddy never has to go away again. And please, God, can we all be together?"

As he listened to his son's earnest plea, Thad felt tears rush down his cheeks. Monica had been right. Peter didn't hate him. He just wanted to be a family.

For a moment, Thad's thoughts flitted to the conversation he'd shared with Monica in the tunnel that led under the sea.

And then he thought about the tunnel, the most secret of all the secret passages, which only he and his father and Monica knew about. And the entrance, which was down the hall in the direction the guards had told him Octavian had taken Monica.

Thad gave Peter and extra squeeze. "Let's go look for Mommy." He trotted back up the hallway in the direction of the throne room and the small storage room where the tunnel entrance was hidden.

Richard and Sheila Miller hurried down the hall toward them.

"Grandpa and Grandma!" Peter squealed excitedly at the sight of two people he knew and trusted.

Thad handed him over. "Take care of Peter. I need to look for Monica."

Richard scooped his grandson into his arms. "If you can bring my daughter back, safe and sound…" He met Thad's eyes, and Thad saw the promise of forgiveness shimmering there.

"I'll do my best," Thad promised.

Thad ran back down the hall and ducked into the small room. A shuffle of footprints on the dusty floor indicated pairs of feet had passed through the space recently, but Thad couldn't be sure whether he and Monica had created the prints the night before, or if they were fresh.

He slid back the wooden jamb to reveal the smaller, more secret room.

"Find anything?" Alec asked behind him.

Thad motioned for his brother to take a look. "This tunnel leads to Dorsi. It has a side branch that leads to a cave that empties out at the cliffs north of the marina."

"Do you think Octavian knew about this tunnel?" Alec looked skeptical. "I didn't even know this was here."

"Father's the only other person who knew about it, until Monica followed me when I went after the scepter."

"*That's* how you got back and forth from Dorsi." Alec put the pieces together. "If Monica knows about the tunnel, she may have led Octavian inside."

Thad pointed through the doorway to where the wall had been slid back, revealing the handle to the trapdoor on the floor. "I left that closed when Monica and I came through. She's been here. I'm nearly certain she led Octavian this way and left it open so we would know."

"I'll get some men. We'll go after them."

"No." Thad grabbed his brother's arm to stop him. "It's highly unstable. The tunnel passes under the sea where the peninsula has been washed away. If we go tromping in there, the sides will most certainly give way. It partially collapsed on me last night. We can't risk further structural damage. Once water breaches the tunnel, it will become a death trap. Monica's in there."

"So what can we do?"

"Dispatch a team to the cliffs north of the marina. That's where the spur empties out. I'll go in after Monica. I have the scepter. Maybe I can arrange a trade."

Alec gave him a doubtful look. "Do you at least have a flashlight?"

Thad realized he didn't, and shook his head.

"Here." Alec slipped a penlight off of his keychain. "Get your wife back."

"Thank you."

Thad slipped quietly down the stairs. Thankfully, the penlight his brother lent him provided just enough light to illumine a couple of steps ahead of him, without giving away his approach. He'd need every advantage he could get over Octavian. The guards had said the tyrant looked ready to shoot. The last thing Thad wanted was for him to get nervous and pull the trigger.

Running, crawling, creeping sideways, Thad moved through the forgotten passage as quickly as he dared. When he reached the intersection where the passage to the cliffs branched off, he paused, shining his light down the side tunnel, looking for any clue that would tell him if Monica and Octavian had gone that way.

But the side passage was void of footprints, and distant echoes hinted at activity ahead of him along the main branch. He headed onward as the tunnel sloped deeper downhill, slowing his pace somewhat. Not only did he not want to let on to Octavian that he was behind them, but he had to be cautious to avoid damaging the tunnel any further.

Already the seeping cracks trickled with streams of water that puddled on the floor. No doubt his excursion the night before had disturbed things. And Octavian's frantic flight was clearly causing additional damage. Thad prayed silently that the corridor would hold up, at least long enough for him to rescue Monica.

As he darted forward, he began to hear noises coming from up ahead. At first he wasn't sure whether he heard trickling water or voices.

Then he realized it was both.

"Maybe we should turn back," Monica suggested to her captor.

"No!" Octavian's fury nearly rattled the walls. "The palace will be teeming with my enemies. We have to go forward."

"But we're underneath the sea. If these walls give way—"

"Then hurry!"

Octavian's voice prodded Thad to move faster. He'd rather risk being heard than arrive too late. Soon he heard splashing up ahead, and came to a low-lying section of tunnel where the water poured through a small crack above, puddling in ever-growing pools on the floor, reaching as high as his ankles in places.

Far ahead, he could see a bouncing light and the

shadows of Octavian and Monica running through the corridor.

There was no point trying to sneak ahead—not if it meant splashing through the puddles. They'd hear him coming. Besides, Thad had no desire to go any farther into the unstable passageway. All he wanted to do was grab Monica and run for the surface.

But first he had to face the enemy who had nearly destroyed his kingdom and his family.

"Octavian!"

The light ahead stopped bouncing.

"I have the scepter!" Thad held it up, shining his brother's penlight on it so Octavian could see clearly that he wasn't bluffing. "You have my wife. Shall we trade?"

Water splashed as Octavian approached.

Was it Thad's imagination, or was the water rushing in even faster now?

His heart slammed inside his chest. The more the sea leaked inward, the more it would push aside the stones. The deluge would only increase. He had to get out of the tunnel. It was a death trap! But he couldn't leave without Monica. Couldn't live with himself if he never got a chance to tell her how much he loved her. And he had to be careful with Octavian. The man had never been trustworthy, and on top of that, he was now desperate.

"You hand me the scepter—" Octavian spoke

slowly as he approached "—and I will give you back your wife."

"Agreed." Thad held out the scepter. He wished Octavian would hurry. They needed to escape. But Octavian approached warily, as though fearing a trap.

Octavian stepped forward cautiously, his gun nearly trembling as he held it under Monica's ribs.

"Please." Thad spoke slowly, smoothly, unwilling for the reverberations of his voice to further upset the delicate balance of the volatile space they occupied. "Take the scepter."

"But if I give you back your wife—" Octavian licked a line of sweat from his upper lip "—how do I know you won't turn around and tackle me? How do I know you don't have more men waiting in the darkness behind you?"

"I'm alone." Thad tried to make his voice soothingly calm. "This tunnel can't withstand any more traffic. We need to get out quickly before the sea rushes in."

"This tunnel is hundreds of years old," Octavian said, shuffling closer through the standing water. "It's not going anywhere."

Thad tried not to let his sense of impatience get the best of him. He moved forward, the scepter extended like an olive branch. If it hadn't been for Octavian's gun, he'd have lunged forward, grabbed Monica and made a run for it back up the tunnel.

But he couldn't risk letting the man get a shot off. Not only was Monica within point-blank range, but firing the weapon would undoubtedly disturb the already fragile corridor. Even if Octavian's shot missed both of them, a single bullet could bury them all in a watery grave.

"Here," Thad said, coming within a couple of meters of Octavian. "Take the scepter." He held it out toward him.

"I believe I will!" Octavian pushed Monica back behind him and lunged forward, gun extended, to nab the scepter from Thad's hands.

Thad realized, a second too late, that Octavian was aiming his weapon at him.

He kicked at the gun just as it went off. The bullet ricocheted off the side wall before slamming into the softer stone of the ceiling. The light of their flashlight beams danced crazily. Octavian's light, by far the stronger of the two, fell to the floor with a splash and went out.

Thad could hardly see. Octavian's hand's closed over the scepter, and Thad tried to pry it from his fingers.

Monica pulled on his arm, tugging him in the direction of the palace, and safety. "Leave it! We've got to run!"

As water poured down from the ceiling, Thad realized she was right. The gun had cracked a fissure in the unstable rock. Already the force of the moving water was shoving the stones apart, widening the stream as the sea sluiced in toward them. They had to leave the scepter behind if they were going to have any chance of getting out of the tunnel alive.

Thad scooped his arm around Monica's waist and ran with her back up the tunnel, his tiny penlight hardly able to illumine the path before they ran through its beam, tearing up the passageway as fast as their legs could carry them.

Behind him, he could hear Octavian's cries over the sound of the rushing water. "The scepter! The scepter!"

"Forget the scepter!" Thad called out as he ran. "Run for your life!"

"Just run!" Monica panted beside him.

The water rose quickly, nearly up to his knees before they reached the section of the tunnel that sloped upward. Still, Thad knew they couldn't risk slowing down.

"This way!" He pulled her in the direction of the cliffside spur. "It reaches high ground more quickly."

They raced upward, panting. A swell of water caught them just as they reached the stairs, its soaking embrace overtaking them, lifting their feet from the floor. For an instant Thad thought they'd be sucked back into the tunnel. But the influx of gushing water pushed them upward, buoying them toward light and air and freedom. Thad kept his mouth closed tight and his arms around Monica as the rising wave carried them upward.

Then the wave receded, beaching them on the rise of steps. Thad scrambled to take hold of the wet stones.

"Are you okay?" Monica panted beside him.

He gulped a breath and tugged her higher up the stairs, in case the rising waters surged upward again. "I'm okay."

She sagged against him, and he wrapped his arms around her, peeling back the wet mat of hair that clung to her forehead.

"There's light ahead." She pointed.

Thad nodded and trudged a few more steps forward before his wet shoes slipped on the steps and he fell forward with her in his arms.

"Monica?" he panted as he searched for her face in the darkness.

"Yes?" She blinked at him, and he realized she'd been right there beside him the whole time.

"I love you." His lips found hers, intending just to leave a light peck there before declaring his intentions to marry her all over again and never leave her side this time.

But somehow, the little kiss became a bigger kiss, and he found himself instead trying to make up for six lost years, kissing her and apologizing and declaring his love. She kissed him back fervently and did the same.

Voices echoed above them.

"Did I hear rushing water?"

"Does this cave lead to the ocean?"

"Let's keep looking."

"No, wait, I see them. There they are!"

"Are they okay?"

"I think so." Kirk's relieved laughter echoed through the cavern. "I think they're finally okay."

Monica held her son on her lap as she waited for the meal to begin. The afternoon had passed by in a crazy scramble of hugs and tears and sodden sneakers. After a quick shower she was finally dry and warm.

Thad entered the dining room, looking handsome and clean shaven. He crossed the room toward her and wrapped one arm round each of them.

Peter looked up at his father with admiration.

"How are my two favorite people in the whole world?"

"Great!" Peter declared.

Monica could hardly speak. She met Thad's eyes, and saw warmth and affection shining back at her. After so long, the man she'd fallen in love with was finally back.

He bent his head toward her ear and murmured quietly, "They've found Octavian's body."

"Inside the tunnel?"

"Apparently the tunnel has washed out completely. His body was found floating in the open sea."

She found his ear, whispering so Peter wouldn't be frightened. "Dead?"

"Yes. He had the scepter inside his jacket."

Monica startled backward and met her husband's eyes.

He smiled at her and raised his voice with a newfound note of triumph. "We got it back. We have everything—the crown, the kingdom…"

"Enough evidence to put all of Octavian's associates away for the rest of their lives," Levi added as he entered the room behind them. "But we'll leave the rest of sorting that out to the courts. This family deserves a celebration." He linked his arm around Isabelle's waist.

"And a celebration it will get," Philip declared as his wife wheeled him into the room.

"Father," Stasi chided him, "don't you need your rest?"

"I've been sleeping for a week." He laughed. "And I've awakened into the happiest dream." He pointed at Peter. "I have a grandson."

Monica had told Peter about the king and queen. Now the boy looked at his grandfather with curiosity. "Are you my other grandpa?"

"Yes." Philip's eyes twinkled happily.

"I thought you were the king," Peter challenged him.

"I was," Philip acknowledged. "But now it's time for your daddy to be king. Would you like that?"

Peter looked up at his father, and then down at Monica. "What about my mommy?"

Monica was about to shush him, to insist she was fine just the way she was, but Thaddeus placed a gentle hand on her shoulder.

"Your mommy will be my queen."

"Will she?" Peter asked.

"I guess it's up to her." Thad met her eyes. Then, apparently uncomfortable standing above her while she sat, he dropped down on one knee and took her hands in his. "They'd like to crown me at noon tomorrow. Would you do me the honor—" His voice caught with emotion, and he squeezed her hand before continuing. "When I am king, will you be my queen?"

Thad hardly made it through the question. Monica cupped his face in her hands and drew him close. "Yes," she whispered just before he kissed her, wrapping his arms around her until she nearly forgot they were not alone.

A roar behind them startled her. She broke away from the kiss to find Thad's siblings and their fiancés cheering with approval. After wondering how his family might receive her, she blushed at their enthusiastic response to the passionate kiss she'd have preferred to keep private.

Thad stood and faced his younger brother and

sisters. "I can think of no better way to begin my reign than with a series of celebrations. And there is no greater celebration than a wedding feast. But, so we don't step on one another's toes, I think you should all work out when you're getting married. Who's going to go first?"

The siblings looked at one another with broad smiles.

"Isabelle was engaged first, so I suppose she should go first," Stasi suggested.

"And Stasi is always late, so I suppose she should go last," Alec declared with a laugh.

Everyone chuckled, until Isabelle spoke up in a sad voice. "But Thaddeus, we all missed your wedding."

A hush fell over the room.

Then Dom Procopio stepped out from where he'd been standing in the corner of the room. "I've been thinking about that. You may have been married for the last six years, but no one in Lydia knew about it. It seems the right and proper thing to do would be to renew your wedding vows tomorrow prior to the coronation."

There was an approving murmur until Stasi asked, "What is Monica going to wear?"

Monica looked up at the wedding portrait of Philip and Elaine, and the classic gown her mother-in-law had chosen for her royal wedding. "I would want it to be something regal and formal, like this." She gestured to the portrait.

"Do you like my dress?" Elaine asked.

"I love it."

"It should fit you nicely." The former queen nodded her approval. "We can try it on this evening and make any necessary alterations, but that can wait. For now, let's eat."

Philip cleared his throat. "Deacon, would you bless the meal?"

"I'd be honored."

As the family bowed their heads around the table, Monica held tight to Peter's hand on one side, and Thad's hand on the other, and gave thanks that God had seen fit to keep her family safe and bring them back together.

EPILOGUE

King Thaddeus of Lydia took his wife's hand and, with a rustle of sashes and silk, pulled her past the milling throngs toward a hallway.

"Thank you." Queen Monica leaned against his shoulder as they walked. "I needed a breath of fresh air. The coronation reception has been overwhelming. I never imagined shaking so many hands—or hugging so many people!"

"They're delighted to have you as their queen." Thad led her around a bend in the hallway. "And they should be. You look radiant. The crown jewels Stasi designed for you are exquisite." He touched the ruby-inlaid crown that graced her head as though she'd been born to wear it. "You're exquisite." His fingers trailed from the crown down her cheek, tilting her chin up to exchange a kiss.

"Mmm, Thad." She kissed him back, then paused. "Did you hear the Sardis University chancellor offer me a teaching position?"

"Is that why you looked so happy chatting with her? I simply thought you'd found a new friend."

"I think we will be friends. But what do you think of the idea of me teaching? Won't my duties as queen preclude that?"

"Your role will be whatever you shape it to be. Now that Octavian is dead and the Royal House of Lydia has reclaimed the crown, you're free to do whatever you like. The most important thing is that you're happy." He kissed her again, amazed at the way every moment with her felt so perfect, and so right.

Monica broke off the kiss just long enough to ask, "Do you think we should check on Peter?"

"Your parents have him. That's where I'm taking you now."

"Where *are* we going?"

"Actually..." Thad hesitated to tell her of his plans. What if she didn't like the surprise? He'd almost told her a dozen times, but he didn't want to spoil the secret. It was a joy, for once, to have a happy secret. "It was my mother's idea. After she and my father were married, they greeted their subjects from this balcony." He opened the door, and together they stepped out onto a wide balcony where their parents, Thad's siblings and their fiancés, and even Monica's sister stood waiting to greet them. Peter reached for his parents and Thad scooped him into his arms as a cheer rose up from below.

"Oh, Thaddeus!" Monica looked down at the crowd spread below. Each person held a candle, and the glowing flames glimmered like a sea of stars in the evening darkness. "Where did you get so many candles?"

Elaine explained, "When Thaddeus disappeared, the people held a candlelight vigil in the courtyard to pray for his safe return. I found the candles in storage while I was getting out my wedding dress."

Candlelight sparkled in the happy tears on Monica's cheeks. Thad wiped them away.

Philip placed a hand on his son's shoulder. "When we prayed you would return to us, we didn't imagine that God would answer our prayers threefold!" The former king looked at Thaddeus, Monica and Peter, and beamed proudly.

Overcome by the emotion of the moment, Thad bent to kiss his wife, and a roar of approval rose from the crowd below. Startled, he pulled away. As Monica reached up and kissed him again, Thaddeus felt the last cold fear melt away from his heart, and he thanked God for bringing them together again.

* * * * *

Dear Reader,

Sometimes what looks like the end is really the beginning. I hope you've enjoyed the story of *The Missing Monarch,* in which the Royal House of Lydia finally reclaims the crown, and the last of the four siblings finds his happily ever after. It's been a long journey, but I've enjoyed sharing every step of it with you.

As it turns out, this isn't the end. In December 2012, Love Inspired Historical will release *A Royal Marriage,* which tells the story of Gisela, daughter of Charlemagne, and the Lydian King John. Learn how the Scepter of Charlemagne first came to Lydia, and how the tiny Kingdom of Lydia survived through some of the darkest years in history.

And keep your eyes out for more stories about the brave men and women you've met in Lydia. You can find news about upcoming releases on my website, www.rachellemccalla.com. Sometimes what looks like the end is really the beginning.

Blessings on your journey,
Rachelle

Questions for Discussion

1. Thad is afraid of getting close to Monica again because he fears Octavian will use his emotions against him. Have you ever felt the need to remain emotionally distant? When is it okay to let our emotions rule us? When is it better to keep our emotions out of things? Can you think of examples in your life when you wished you'd remained objective? Are there times when you should have given in to what you felt? How do those experiences influence your current attitudes and relationships?

2. Monica's trip to the Arctic Circle to find Thad feels to her like flying out of the range of the eyes of God. But then she recalls Psalm 24, which says, "The earth is the Lord's, and everything in it." Have you ever been in such a dark place that it felt as though God wasn't there? Did you carry God's light into that dark place? Or did you find it was already shining there?

3. The villain Octavian has wreaked havoc in the lives of Thad's siblings and endangered all of Lydia. How do the events of Octavian's youth help us to understand how he became the way he is? Do you know any people who remind you of Octavian?

4. Thad can't imagine Monica forgiving him for abandoning her. When Thad apologizes, she forgives him without hesitation. How does her attitude toward the small things open his heart up to the possibility of forgiveness over much larger infractions? What does your attitude about the little things tell people about your willingness to forgive? What little steps can you take today to communicate a forgiving attitude toward those you love?

5. All the members of the royal family played an important part in protecting the kingdom of Lydia. How does your family or circle of close friends work together for the good of the kingdom? In what ways do trials and difficult experiences make you stronger as a family of faith?

6. No one was sure whether General Marc Petrela could be trusted. Even though the general knew they didn't trust him, he continued to be faithful to the crown. What do you think about his character? Would you have trusted him? Do you agree with the way Thad and Monica dealt with the uncertain role of his presence among them?

7. Thad observes that Octavian's motto seems to be "If at first you don't succeed, try something more evil." Have you ever felt tempted to take revenge on those who have wronged you? How

do you get over those experiences and move your life in a positive direction?

8. When Thad and Monica get lost in Sardis, they find a high hill in an attempt to see the way home. At the same time, Monica wishes Thad could find his way back to the faith that had sustained him as a child. Have you ever been a long way from home, and needed to find your way back? Do you have loved ones who are far from home? How can you illumine the path for them?

9. Nearly through their two-day allotment of time, Monica feels as though she's farther away from her goal than ever. She suspects this is precisely how Octavian wants her to feel. Have you ever felt as though you're moving backward, messing up everything you're trying to fix? How did Monica get over her discouraged feelings? Can you move forward in spite of the lies your enemies whisper in your ears? What steps can you take to overcome them?

10. Thad refuses to pray because he thinks God won't answer him anyway. But as he softens to the idea, he finds comfort knowing that others are praying for him. Is there anyone you care about whose attitude resembles Thad's? Does his story encourage you to keep praying?

11. When Thaddeus places his hand in a crack in the tunnel, he discovers that the entire stone structure shifts constantly. This, he concludes, is the secret to its long survival: it is not brittle, but flexible. What parallels can you identify between the flexibility of the tunnel, and human flexibility? Where did Thad need to learn to "give way" in order to stay strong?

12. Monica is afraid that her son will be influenced by Octavian, and she prays that the solid foundation she's laid in his life will get him through his experience. Are there young people in your life for whom you can help provide a solid faith foundation? What steps can you take to give them a faith that won't be shaken?

13. When Thaddeus learns that his son looks up to him and loves him, he's afraid Peter will only be disappointed once he meets him. Have you ever let the fear of spoiling something nice keep you from reaching for something great? If Thad had settled for preserving Peter's impression of him by staying away from his son, what might he have missed out on?

14. When the sea is crashing in upon them, Thad and Monica urge Octavian to leave the scepter behind and run for his life. Consider Octavian's

choice in the light of these verses from Mark 8:35–36, "For whoever wants to save their life will lose it, but whoever loses their life for me and for the gospel will save it. What good is it for someone to gain the whole world, yet forfeit their soul?"

15. As Thad and Monica are trying to escape the dark tunnel, he looks for her and realizes she's been right there beside him the entire time. In what ways is the love you seek already there with you? Have you ever found God walking so closely beside you that you forgot He was even there? What can you do today to embrace the love that has been offered to you?